---

# BRIGHT LIGHTS

The Spies Who Loved Her Prequel Interlude

---

## KATRINA JACKSON

one

"We're going to lose our deposit."

"We won't lose our deposit."

"We're not allowed to hang pictures on the wall. Why do you think management is going to let this fly?"

"Ken Doll," Chanté said, exasperated, "I already told you, I know a guy—"

"Who knows a guy who can hack into management and make it look like we already paid this month's rent. Yeah, I know, I know."

She turned to him and rolled her eyes. "Actually, I could do that myself, but plausible deniability and all that. What I was actually going to say is that the cook at the club works in construction, and he told me that he'd come by and fix any damage we do and paint and stuff for seventy-five bucks flat when we move out. Holes included."

As she spoke, her voice rose to a high-pitched squeak like it sometimes did when she was worked up in some way. She used to hate it, but over the years, she'd learned how to wield it like a weapon. Who could say no to Chanté when her voice broke adorably? Almost no one, she'd learned. Who could deny Chanté her heart's desire when she smiled and showed her dimples? Even fewer. A few years in a group home because her parents couldn't get their shit together had taught Chanté that every skill had to be sharpened like a blade because she was the only thing she could control. And of all the things she didn't have, the lack of a safety net was the one that loomed over her like her own personal rain cloud.

But Chanté didn't have time to get lost in a storm. She was made of pure sunshine, and she never let herself — or anyone else — forget it.

Unfortunately, her roommate and best friend in the making, Kenny, was one of those few people who were immune to her squeak *and* smile. He was the warmest, softest center encased in a hard shell of corded muscle, great hair, and a chiseled jaw, and a sugar coating made of pure skepticism. Try as she might, she'd never been able to break through all that practicality, but she would live to try again.

"And what happens when that cook goes back to jail?" Kenny asked, hands on his hips, very suburban dad-like in his demeanor. He was an adorable downer as usual.

"First of all, George has been straight and clean since he got out of the pen last year. Second of all, his son also does construction, and he likes me, so I think we're good. Always have a backup," Chanté trilled. "Now, will you please help me put this heavy ass pole in place?"

She abandoned the squeak and huffed out her request for Kenny's assistance a second time. Thankfully, this time he came to her rescue, deftly picking up the dance pole and holding it vertically as if it weighed nothing. Maybe to him, it didn't.

"Here?" he asked, holding the pole in place in the center of their living room.

"Yeah. Yeah. Right here," she said, scrambling onto one of their dining chairs with their handheld drill in her left hand to drill it into place.

It was a testament to their perfect harmony as friends and roommates that Chanté wanting to erect a pole to practice her exotic dancing in their living room wasn't more of a kerfuffle beyond the way it might affect their deposit. To be fair, they barely used the living room for much. Kenny was usually in class or at his part-time job at the grocery store. He came home to eat, sleep, or watch a couple of episodes of *Alias* with Chanté as their roommate bonding activity for the week, but those were rare occasions.

Chanté was in the apartment more, but not by much. When she wasn't in class, she was at the strip club where she waitressed. If she had a free evening, instead of hanging at home, she called down to the club to pick up extra shifts, putting her extra funds to work covering the deep chasm between her scholarship funds and the money she actually needed to live. But even when she wasn't covering for one of the other waitresses, Chanté would stop by just to watch the girls on stage; much more entertaining than whatever was on primetime tv.

Chanté considered the hours she spent at the club studying her favorite dancers almost as important — maybe even more on some days — as the time she spent studying for her degree, and she approached them in the same way: focused study, detailed note-taking, and dedicated practice. Or at least, she was supposed to be practicing. In reality, she'd been thinking about practicing, choreographing a series of routines for her future performances in her head, and telling herself that she'd perfect them...someday. Except, someday wasn't coming fast enough.

That's why she'd bought the pole.

One night, a customer had gotten really drunk and tipped her better than normal for just ferrying his whiskey and wings from the bar to his table quickly and because she "had the best ass in the place," which was true, and he thought she "should be up there shaking it." That was also true, so she'd used his unexpected but very appreciated bounty to invest in her future.

"Okay, the top's secure," she said, locking the pole in place. "Let me do the bottom, and we're good."

"They're gonna notice these holes," Kenny said.

"Management didn't know there wasn't a toilet seat when we moved in until you told them. I think we're good." She hopped down from the chair and started securing the first of three screws into the carpeted floor.

"What about the people who live above us?"

"Stoners, up and down. I asked them if they cared already."

"You did?"

"Of course. It would have been rude not to. Upstairs said they didn't care and slammed the door in my face. Downstairs said it was cool and sold me some edibles."

He rolled his eyes. "This building is ridiculous."

"But very affordable," she said, turning the last screw.

"And you're sure this is safe?"

"Absolutely."

"What if you're wrong?" he asked adorably.

"What if the world ends tomorrow?"

"That's not a proper response," he shot back, trying to shake the pole to see if it would hold now that it was bolted into place. "Don't use this when you're home alone. Just in case."

"Is that your way of asking me to dance for you?"

He huffed out a laugh that would have hurt Chanté if she wanted to be with him for real, but she didn't. She loved flirting with him, though; loved the way his face turned bright red like he'd had a drink, and his normally strong, confident, deep voice turned shaky and high-pitched. Caleb called her a shameless tease, and he was right. Most times, Chanté flirted for the hell of it, and when it came to Kenny, the hell of it was better than success.

"Not to be rude, but I see you dancing in next to no clothing four or five times a week for free, no matter how many times I ask you to *not* do that. You didn't need to buy a pole."

"First of all, you're welcome for the friend discount," she said, pulling a heavy burst of laughter from him, and that was even better than his embarrassment.

He turned to her with a smile on his face and reached out to give her shoulders a firm, reassuring squeeze. "I just don't want you to fall and bust your head open. Management will definitely draw the line at blood," he said, a sliver of worry flashing across his face.

Chanté smiled up at him. Kenny was a great friend, and he'd be prime DILF material someday.

"No dancing on the pole while you're here alone," he said, "at least at first. Okay?"

She wanted to tease him, but she couldn't. Even with lots of therapy, Chanté positively blossomed under the love and attention of people who loved her, especially if she loved them back, and she didn't want Kenny to think she didn't appreciate his concern. "Fine," she mumbled. "I'll hold off until we can schedule a time for me to dance for you."

"Not for me," Kenny corrected in exasperation. "Just with me in the apartment."

"Watching me," she teased, bumping his leg with her hip.

"Watching over you. Aren't you about to be late for your shift?"

Chanté's eyes squinted at his diversion. She lifted her wrist to peer at her watch. "Oh, shit!" she yelped, throwing the drill on the couch as she sprinted toward her bedroom.

"Hey, can you bring some wings back for me?" he called after her.

"They're not good when you microwave them," she yelled from her room, pulling her t-shirt over her head and kicking off her sweatpants. She grabbed her shortest pair of jean shorts and a crop top from her dresser and started to dress with her bedroom door wide open, once again giving Kenny the kind of view she wanted to charge premium prices for at the club.

He sighed in return. She could hear him cleaning up her mess in the living room.

"You gotta put them in the oven," Kenny called back.

Chanté rushed back into the living room, shoving her tallest but still kind of comfortable heels into her backpack alongside her ISS textbook. "For real?" she asked.

"For real."

She zipped up her bag and slipped on the worn pair of Chuck Taylors she wore nearly every day and kept by the front door. "Okay. I'll bring some back."

"You're the best," Kenny called after her as she rushed out of their apartment.

"I know!" she yelled back just as their door swung closed.

CHANTÉ LOVED PLAYLISTS. She used to rip all of her favorite songs from P2P sites to make her ultimate annual best-of lists and share them with her friends scattered around foster and group homes around Detroit, and she had continued the project in college, regularly sending burned CD playlists home to her friends or uploading them to her blog for Caleb to download.

Kenny teased her about it, but if she didn't slip a

CD-R to him at the end of the semester, he pouted until she burned him a copy. She was busy a lot with work and school, but the club was a great place to hear the latest hip-hop and R&B cuts, and sometimes, she used her bus rides to audition new songs. Today, she was auditioning "Adorn" by Miguel since she knew Caleb had a crush on the singer. As soon as she climbed onto the bus, she pressed her earbuds into her ears and pressed play, letting the song wash over her as the city passed her by.

The ride from Chanté's co-op off-campus apartment to the club where she worked was like what her urban history professor, Dr. James, might have described as the literal embodiment of American economic and racial inequality. At least three nights a week — sometimes five — Chanté sat in the front of the bus with her earbuds in, watching the landscape of the city change so drastically that she often had a hard time believing she hadn't travelled to a different county or country.

The farther her bus moved from campus, the more the concrete narrowed and cracked. Chanté could see the wear and tear of life and the elements on every sidewalk and building, and no reinvestment of the community's tax dollars. There, neglect seemed to spread from the ground up. The buildings became more rundown, with broken windows and litter scattered along the ground because whoever worked the garbage route in this neighborhood didn't care if they dumped more trash in the gutter than they collected.

Chanté didn't need her textbook to know that something like that would never have happened closer to campus in the neighborhoods with million-dollar houses owned by university professors and administrators. Near campus, the bus couldn't go more than two stops before she spotted another grocery store of a slightly different stripe — Whole Foods, Trader Joe's, the vegan fresh market that Chanté and Kenny didn't even think about going to because they couldn't afford anything in there. But the closer she got to work, there were fewer grocery stores, until eventually, there were only just corner stores and payday loan spots. She knew nearly everyone who worked in those storefronts, and when her student loan payment was due, and money was *really* tight, she knew she could buy her groceries at the corner store across the street from the club. Their food was a little dodgy, but okay in a pinch, and Chanté was always in a pinch, especially between semesters.

Chanté knew this bus trip so well because it was like the bus trips she used to make in high school, traveling from school in the slightly better part of town to a succession of foster houses on the decidedly worse parts of town. When she sat in Dr. James's lecture on "urban blight," she'd recognized the images of cities from all over the country as her own. In fact, she'd gripped her pen when a picture of a neighborhood in Detroit she knew *very* well flashed on the screen. She'd been so arrested by the image that she'd missed part of the lecture and had to slink up to the front of the class-room to ask for the slides, nervously admitting that she'd been distracted by seeing her hometown onscreen. She'd been afraid of what Dr. James would say, dreading the response when she revealed a part of herself she wasn't actually ashamed of, but she knew some people thought she should hide. She hadn't expected to hear his lecturer voice slip away and a thick Detroit accent to greet her. She could still remember the relief that had coursed through her.

Her bus ride to work was so textbook that she'd been working up the nerve to propose using it for her final observation paper in Dr. James's class. It would make a great case study. The only thing tripping her up was exposing herself. She didn't mind writing the paper for Dr. James, but the thought of her final presentation made her stomach clench with worry about her classmates. She couldn't imagine exposing not just her past but her present to people who wouldn't understand that not everyone had enrolled with a personal letter of recommendation from someone on the state Supreme Court. Some people had to work to pay their tuition and buy books on a severe budget. She didn't have any faith in her elitist classmates being open to the revolutionary idea that people like Chanté were the majority, not the minority, at their private college. And since her part-time job was serving drinks at a strip club where she really wanted to dance, she also doubted that the other working-class students would stand with her.

Except Kenny, and probably Dr. James, but two people wasn't enough. No, she'd just have to think of a different paper topic, no matter how perfect this one was.

"Ain't this your stop comin' up?" the driver, Miss Francine, asked.

Chanté spotted the club through the bus's front window. She pressed the call button and stood. She slipped her backpack on and paused her music.

"You get on that stage yet?" Miss Francine asked.

"Not yet. I'm still not ready to audition," Chanté said, leaning against the partition between the front stairwell and the rest of the bus.

Miss Francine usually told her to find a seat and park her butt when she tried to stand here unless she was about to get off, and Chanté always took advantage. Ever since she was a kid, she'd loved to look out of the front window of a large city bus. There was something about seeing a street through that window that made Chanté feel as if the world was bigger than she imagined but much more manageable than feared. Sometimes, she thought about what it would be like to have the kind of control bus drivers needed to operate such a large machine so carefully. She wanted to exert that kind of control over her future. She was desperate for it, actually.

"Whatchu mean, you not ready? From what I heard, they still letting Sherri get her grasshopper-looking ass up there even though she sprained both her ankles walking onstage that one time. You can do better than that!"

Chanté ducked her head to giggle. "She was out of commission for like three months. Saraiya banned her from wearing anything more than a kitten heel."

Miss Francine tsked and shook her head as she pulled along the curb and slowed the bus to a stop. "Damn shame. Bet she still making good money, though."

"She sure is," Chanté breathed, thinking about what her life would be like if she was pulling that kind of cash.

The bus doors opened, and Chanté bounced down the stairs before anyone could get on.

"How many times I gotta tell you the exit is at the back?" Miss Francine called, her voice only lightly annoyed.

"Just a couple more times, I promise," Chanté trilled.

"Mmmhmm. See you tonight, Miss Thang."

"Yes, ma'am," Chanté waved. She turned her music back on and headed toward the club.

When she'd gotten the job waitressing at The Petal, Caleb had insisted on some serious sleuthing about the club and the surrounding neighborhood, finding the closest police station — so she could avoid it — and every security camera he could find for potential hacking purposes, just in case. The kind of barely legal — or downright illegal — hacking that she'd sworn off while she got an actual computer science degree.

She and Caleb had grown up in the same group homes but had taken wildly divergent paths toward their futures. Her best friend bought a one-way plane ticket to New York for his eighteenth birthday and had never looked back except to keep an eye out for Chanté. In that vein, he'd hacked into her university's housing database to assign her a single room, even though she'd paid for a triple. Chanté *could* have done that — but didn't — because she was trying to go straight, but she was no fool. She'd taken Caleb's gift and prepared to act shocked when the error was discovered. It was nice to know that somewhere — maybe New York, maybe L.A., maybe D.C. — Caleb was watching out for her. It wasn't a safety net per se, but it was something.

Chanté ducked into the alleyway that led to the employee entrance that was really just a fire door on the side of the building. Technically, they weren't supposed to use that door for this purpose, but since the city inspector didn't seem to care, why should they? That was the logic the club used, at least.

Chanté balled up her fist and pounded it against the metal door, and jumped out of the way as Stevie, head of security, pushed it open.

"Good evening, Chanté," he said, motioning for her to come inside.

"Hey. How's the crowd?" she asked.

Stevie leaned out into the alleyway to make sure nothing looked out of place before pulling the door firmly shut. "Rowdy," he said, answering her question. "Bunch of dipshits from your school."

"How you know they from my school?"

"Grammar," Stevie said.

Chanté rolled her eyes. "How do you know they're from my school?" she said, smiling up at the older man who patrolled the club like it was the last line of defense for Homeland Security, and the dancers, waitresses, and bartenders inside were the First Family.

"Better," he said, motioning for Chanté to follow him down the hallway. "I know they are from your university because they showed up in university sweatshirts. You know, in my day—" he started, but Chanté laughed and cut him off.

"No. I just got here. You are not telling me about all the strip clubs you've visited in your life."

He smiled down at her. "Not *all*. Just the ones with a dress code," he teased.

"The Petal has a uniform," she said, looking down at her tight shorts and crop top, covered by a jean jacket.

"Not for the workers," Stevie said, "for the customers. That's how you know you're in a classy place."

"Hate to break it to you, but The Petal is not classy. Fabulous, yes, but classy? Absolutely not."

Stevie sighed. "Could be if Saraiya would listen to me."

"I am not getting in the middle of this. Way above my pay grade. My shift is starting soon, anyway."

Stevie sighed again. "Well, go on, then. I'll tell you about my plans some other time."

Chanté smiled and waved. "I know you will. See you on the floor."

He nodded and waved at her, leaving her at the locker room for floor staff. Down the hall, she could just see the door to the dancers' locker room. The door was always closed to give the dancers privacy, but sometimes Chanté got lucky when she was walking down the hallway and caught a glimpse inside just as the door was swinging closed. Sometimes, her brain would slow that peek from seconds to hours just so she could take it all in; the flash of sequins in the warm fluorescent light, neon Lycra hugging brown skin, the waterfall of wavy weave down a long back. It was the best view in the world as far as Chanté was concerned.

Chanté got a job at The Petal before her freshman year of college started on a bit of a whim.

She'd been eighteen with two and half years' experience working the cash register at McDonald's, which was just enough experience to know that she never wanted to work in a fast-food restaurant again. She'd been applying for waitressing or cashier jobs when she passed by The Petal. Saraiya was posting a flyer outside for help, and Chanté had asked for an application before her future boss had finished taping the notice on the front door. That was her tenth application that day, and she would have forgotten about it nearly as soon as she'd handed the paper over, except The Petal was the only place she'd applied to that still had paper job applications. She'd also gone the wrong way out of Saraiya's office and ended up in this same hallway only to see inside that door for a brief moment as it swung closed, and she'd known immediately that working at The Petal was her dream job. Standing in that hallway that day had made her feel the same way she'd felt when she'd learned how to hack into the library's system to wipe the overdue fines she'd accumulated hoarding copies of Eric Jerome Dickey novels.

"Keep daydreamin', and you gone be late," Angie said, brushing past Chanté into the locker room.

"I'm not daydreaming," Chanté said, following her inside.

"Yeah, you are. You're always daydreaming, but tonight is not the night."

"Stevie said the crowd is rowdy." Chanté pulled open the first free locker she found. She toed off her shoes and pulled her socks off. She shoved them in the bottom of the locker and then pulled her heels from her backpack.

"They're not rowdy, just annoying. Frat boys," she said with a roll of her eyes and a frown. "They're tipping okay, though."

"Good to know."

Angie held her pack of cigarettes in the air and smiled. "See you out there after my break."

Chanté nodded and slipped carefully into her heels, making sure the ankle strap was nice and secure. She checked her watch. Three minutes before her shift started. She used a full minute to allow her feet time to adjust to the heels, walking in circles around the locker room. Some people hated heels, but Chanté was five feet tall barefoot. She preferred to view the world from the vantage point of average height if given the choice. When her feet were ready, she pulled the lock from her backpack, slammed the locker closed, and walked carefully toward the main room of the club.

She forced herself not to look down the hall toward the dancers' room because Angie was right; she was always daydreaming about what it would be like to be on stage while working the floor. It was easy to get caught up in that fantasy, but she needed to break out of that. She needed to live in reality, and in reality, she wasn't a dancer. Not yet, at least. She'd taken this job over the Denny's because Denny's didn't have the stage, and The Petal did, and she should be taking advantage of it.

Sometimes, Chanté dreamt about the stage; the hazy smoke in the room, the pole gleaming in the lights, the bass from the music vibrating through her heels and up her legs. She liked to imagine herself there whenever she had a free moment, but she'd gotten too comfortable in her dreams. She needed to take a step into the future. Besides, Miss Francine thought she was ready, Chanté reminded herself.

"Here you are," Saraiya said from behind the bar. "You're almost late."

Chanté gave Saraiya her best smile. "Almost doesn't count," she squeaked.

Saraiya rolled her eyes and nodded toward the main floor.

When Chanté turned, her eyes skipped across the expanse of small round tables at the center of the room. Stevie was right; nearly all the people she saw were wearing some Cleveland University shirt or sweatshirt.

"Take the booths," Saraiya said loud enough for Chanté to hear over the music.

"Thank you," Chanté whispered.

Saraiya winked and shooed her away.

Chanté straightened her back, took a deep breath, and took one confident step on a too-tall heel toward her customers.

People who thought waitressing was mindless work had either never done it, weren't good at it, or were assholes. Chanté knew it was an art form, and she considered every shift an opportunity to hone her skills. She kept her eyes forward but alert, and she walked as if she was on a narrowed winding runway.

Her first few weeks at the club, she'd been so terrible at working the floor that Saraiya had almost fired her. She'd tripped over customers' feet, bumped into girls giving lap dances, and even spilled half a pint of beer on the stage, which could have killed one of the dancers. Her tips had been atrocious.

More than once, she'd considered quitting, trying to head off her eventual firing, only to find herself right back at the club with the kind of stubborn determination that most people assumed Chanté didn't — or couldn't — possess. A year later, Chanté was confident but not cocky. She made sure to avoid any unwanted bumps or knocks and stayed well out of the way of any errant hands shooting out to grab at her. She walked toward the row of booths along the east wall with the kind of confidence that came from practice.

The booths could be a blessing or a curse,

depending on the night. Some nights the local businessmen would hold the booths hostage, pretending to bond with their coworkers and talk business, while their eyes darted around the club looking for their favorite dancers. Those assholes never tipped. The best nights were when they showed up with foreign businessmen they wanted to impress and let the bills rain down on the dancers. Even the waitresses walked out with a healthy all-cash take then. Chanté rounded the corner to the first booth praying for a good night. Rent was due soon, she'd need a new computer soon, and her scholarship didn't cover summer classes. She needed a windfall. She always needed a windfall.

What she found when she stood in front of the first booth tucked away in the farthest, darkest corner of the bar was dark curls that made her think of midnight and a smirk that made her feel as if she'd been stripped naked already.

"Wow," she breathed before she could catch herself.

## two

"What's it like in there?" Smith asked in Asif's ear.

Asif took a sip of water from the cup in front of him and tried to ignore the other man's voice intruding on this attempt to case the club, which was hard as it was. Not because of all the flesh — although he appreciated that — but trying to keep track of potential threats in a near-pitch black bar with strobe lights was the worst-case scenario. The overhead lights were meant to focus everyone's attention on the stage, leaving the rest of the club dim, which made it nearly impossible to see the part of the room he most needed and had the added benefit of making him stand out for looking anywhere else but at the woman currently crawling up the pole on center stage. In essence, Smith was adding an unnecessary complication to an already tough job, and Asif wanted to throttle him.

This was why Asif hated wearing earpieces. Saying it was his least favorite part of his job might have been an overstatement since he'd been shot a few times, but still. Asif hated having strangers' voices in his head, drowning out his own thoughts. In this job, he only had himself. Sure, The Agency liked to pretend that wasn't the case to get people to trust their backup and support staff, but none of his support staff had taken any of those bullets for him. Besides, Asif was good at this job precisely because when push came to shove, his heart rate slowed, his brain settled, and he followed his instincts to do what needed to be done and get out of sticky situations alive. But with Smith in his ear, he was having a hard time getting into the right headspace to do his job.

Smith was only one complication, however. There was also his suit, expensive but too tight around the shoulders. Even the soda water he was sipping was a distraction. What he wanted was a drink to dull the sound of Smith's voice in his ear and the nerves he was currently pretending he didn't feel, but alcohol would only make surveillance that much harder, maybe impossible. At least the show on stage was a distraction he'd expected.

Basically, his very first mission as a full-fledged agent was going to shit before it even started.

"Can you expense a lap dance?" Smith asked.

"Shut up," Asif muttered under his breath.

"I'm just asking, so we're prepared."

"*We* don't need to be prepared for that," Asif said. "You're not in here."

"I should have been, though," Smith said, settling into a full-blown conversation over what was supposed to be a secure, closed line of communication used to convey only the most vital information to an agent in the field.

Asif exhaled loudly and pulled his earpiece from his ear, tucking it under the collar of his dress shirt. It was against protocol to sever communication with backup, and Asif could be written up for it, but he didn't care. He wasn't a snitch, but if anyone had a problem with what he'd done, he was all too happy to relay this entire conversation as a rebuttal. But that was a problem for another day.

Now that Smith was out of his ear, Asif took a deep breath and began to scan the room efficiently. Or at least, he tried to. As soon as he settled into the seemingly casual perusal, a pair of tits in a white too-tight crop top t-shirt and an adorable, slightly rounded stomach moved into his line of sight, obscuring his view of the room. Asif frowned and slowly lifted his eyes to a face that was, objectively, the best he'd ever seen. Small, round, with an adorable button nose, big brown eyes, long eyelashes, and plump, glossy lips curved into a nervous smile.

She was beautiful.

"Welcome to The Petal. Can I get you something to drink?"

Asif tilted his head to the right.

One of The Agency's first lessons was not to rush into an answer — any answer. Very few situations required an immediate response, and if it did, there were probably weapons involved. In those situations, the answer was often surprisingly unimportant. That was a lesson he took to heart, especially in this moment when it was more than a pleasure just to look.

"What can I get you to drink?" he asked.

Instead of frowning, her lips puckered and shifted to the left, her button nose wrinkling along the bridge in confusion. "Huh?"

He shifted in his seat, crossing his legs at the knee under the table, lacing his fingers together, and settling his hands in his lap. He pressed his chest forward before he spoke. "This place has a two-drink minimum, does it not?"

She nodded.

"Then you shouldn't ask a customer *if* you can get them something to drink. Don't give people any wiggle room to cheat you; they'll always take it."

She chewed her bottom lip and frowned slightly. "Are you the new owner?" she asked in a squeak. He was focused so intently on her mouth, even though he should have been looking at her eyes.

"What would make you think that?" he asked.

"Um… Saraiya told us last week that the new owner might do an audit, and—" She took a deep breath and sighed on the exhale as her frown deepened.

Asif finally lifted his gaze to her big doll eyes and found them shimmering wet with tears. Some men thought the sight of a woman crying was attractive; they said it activated some latent protective instinct in their DNA. Asif thought that was bullshit. Watching shimmering tears fill this woman's eyes made Asif uncomfortable. He wanted to shove her inside a suit of armor and give her every gun he had on his body; he did not revel in this sight.

"Don't cry," he said in a sharp bark that made her jump where she stood. He sighed. "I'm sorry. I shouldn't have yelled at you."

She swiped at her plump round cheeks with both hands and shook her head. "You're going to fire me, aren't you?"

"Because you're crying?"

"Yes. Who wants to come to a strip club to watch a waitress cry?"

"I'm sure someone does," he said with an easy shrug that he hoped masked the way his eyes were traveling over her body, across the swell of her chest, across the expanse of her bared stomach and the dangling jeweled ring in her belly button, from one wide hip to another, and finally, to the sight of her thick thighs, stretching the fabric of her shorts near to bursting. He let his eyes linger there, imagining slipping his index finger under the hem of those shorts, lightly scratching at her soft skin. He wondered if she would squeak when she moaned.

"I memorized the number to OSHA," she said, her voice suddenly hard as flint.

When Asif's eyes moved back up her body to her face, her tears were gone. Her face was still round and soft and warm, and somehow, her mouth looked even softer now, but her eyes were hard and shooting daggers his way.

"I'm not your new boss."

"I don't believe you. You're probably just saying that so I don't report you for harassment."

Asif smiled so wide that his eyes nearly closed. "Good girl," he said.

She crossed her arms over her chest and frowned down at him. "That's an inappropriate response for the workplace."

He needed to nip this conversation in the bud immediately. Every second he spent engaging in this comedy of errors with his waitress was a second he risked his target showing up and him missing it. Hell, his target could be shimmying her way up the pole on the main stage right now, and he wouldn't have any idea. He needed to cut this conversation off, but he didn't.

"Assuming I was your boss—"

"I'm convinced you are now," she said, cutting him off and shifting her weight onto her left leg. She was glaring down at him now. He liked it.

"*Assuming* I *was* your boss, I would think that reassuring you when you've done a good job would be a good thing."

"That's what you would say if you were trying not to get sued."

Asif pressed his lips together to stop from smiling too much. "I agree."

"You…do?"

"I do." He smiled up at her. "And if I were your boss, I'd tell you that if you feel the need to cry, you can leave the floor and do so in private."

The waitress's face relaxed, and she uncrossed her arms. "Okay… I believe you now."

Asif's eyebrows lifted.

"They're cool here, but they don't like us to leave the floor unless we're covered in liquor or…worse."

Asif burst into a soft laugh. "And you haven't called OSHA about that?"

She shrugged. "I need the job."

"You're too young to be so cynical."

She squinted at him. "I don't need to be thirty to need a job."

"True, but you're young. You could find another

job, surely? Someplace where you can cry in peace, at least."

She turned and looked behind her.

The part of Asif's brain that hadn't forgotten that he was here to work kicked into gear, and he shifted to look behind her, performing a quick scan around the room, looking for the target and monitoring the exits. Nothing. His eyes shifted to the waitress's face and followed her line of sight to the stage, where a woman in a strappy white pleather bodysuit was currently hanging upside down on a pole by the strength of her thighs and calves. She was turning slowly, winking at the audience that was appropriately throwing bills onto the stage below her.

"Ah," he said softly.

She turned back to him, ducking her head to bite back her smile. "I'm in college," she said. "I need the extra money."

"You could make more up there than down here, right?"

She nodded eagerly.

"So, what are you doing threatening me instead of emptying my wallet up there?"

She bit her bottom lip and shoved her hands into the back pockets of her shorts. Adorable. Innocent.

"I'm, um… I'm too nervous to audition," she admitted in a soft voice that made him lean forward to catch each syllable.

They locked eyes, and Asif let himself sink into the depths of her gaze. Any thought of ending this conversation flew from his head. What mission?

"What do you have to be nervous about?" he asked.

She shrugged. "I've just never…you know…danced before. On stage, I mean. I'm not ready," she added hastily.

"I hear practice makes perfect."

She rolled her eyes at him with a smile. "Duh. I'm…working on it. You know?"

"Are you?"

"Yeah," she said excitedly. "I just bought my own pole so I can practice at home."

Asif lifted an eyebrow at her as a hunger he'd never known appeared out of nowhere and seeped into his veins. He wanted to see her on that pole, and it roared through him. "Is that right?" he asked in a whisper.

She sucked in a breath and nodded slowly.

"Well, if you need a practice audience," he offered, even though he shouldn't have. He couldn't ever make good on this offer, and yet he let it dangle in the air, hoping she would grasp onto it. To him.

"If you were my boss, this would be completely inappropriate," she whispered back.

"But I'm not your boss, remember?"

"Who are you?"

He shrugged and shook his head. He couldn't

answer that — not truthfully, at least — but try as it might, his brain couldn't call to mind the cover he'd spent the last week memorizing front to back. His brain stuttered as he tried to grasp onto any part of his fake identity, and she watched him with wide eyes, gently parted mouth, and softly heaving chest.

"Chanté, you better get moving. If the new owner's here, you don't want them to see you standing still," another waitress said as she passed by his table.

Asif watched as his waitress, Chanté, sucked in a sharp breath and looked around the room, seeming to come to her senses. He wished he could say the same.

When she looked back at him, her face was back to that soft, round, open expression she'd been wearing when she'd interrupted his scan of the room. Ah, he thought, that was her "tip me good" face. He bet it was effective.

"What can I get you to drink?" she squeaked at him.

"Cranberry juice."

She squinted. "Really?"

"Really. I don't drink." He hated lying to her.

"Okay. Cranberry juice, coming right up." She smiled and turned away.

"Thank you, Chanté," he said, carefully wrapping his mouth around her name.

Her steps faltered, and she looked at him over her right shoulder. She licked her lips, and he licked his own in return. He watched as she walked slowly to the next booth. In fact, he kept his eyes on her as she moved down the line of booths along the wall, riveted. Absentmindedly, he moved his earpiece back to his ear, knowing that he needed to check in with Smith. He prepared himself to hear the other man going apoplectic on the other end of the connection.

Instead, his backup was prattling on about the last time he'd been to a strip club.

"…so, the twins had this routine that involved dry ice and lasers…"

Asif rolled his eyes and pulled his earpiece out again. His eyes moved around the room. He should have been scanning the crowd for his target like he was supposed to, but he was looking for Chanté instead.

Before he could find his waitress, his target walked into the room. Asif's breathing slowed, his brain settled, and he moved his earpiece back into place. He was ready to do what needed to be done. Asif settled into his seat and trained his face toward the stage casually, while his eyes followed his target across the room to a booth just to the left of the main stage, conveniently in Asif's direct line of sight. He moved his earpiece back to his ear. "Target acquired," he whispered to Smith.

Thankfully, the man stopped speaking. Finally.

----

three

----

"You really gotta appreciate Kay's dedication to choreographing a set for every Rihanna single ever," Chanté
said, her eyes riveted to the stage, where Kay, the
undisputed Petal headliner, was wrapping her body
around the pole to "Birthday Cake" while dressed like
a cupcake. As usual, Chanté wondered how much she
spent on her costumes; it had to be a fortune.

"The hell I do," Angie said with a disgusted grunt.
"You know how many times I've heard this damn song
this week?"

The two women were pressed into a corner of the
bar. Saraiya was backstage making sure the lineup for
the rest of the night was set, so Chanté and Angie were
taking a break to enjoy the show for a few minutes.
Usually, Chanté took full advantage of any moment to
watch the dancers on stage or working the floor, care-

fully observing their routines and techniques, and lying to herself that one day, that would be her out there deftly offering her garter to a customer after negotiating the price of a lap dance. She'd practiced it so many times in her head that it felt real, but it wasn't. No matter how many pep talks she gave herself, she couldn't shake the feeling that she needed to know just a little bit more before she was ready to shoot her shot.

Tonight, however, her attention was divided between the dancers she admired and her customer with the dark hair and eyes and an earnestly filthy grin.

"He look like he got money," Angie whispered into her ear.

Chanté blushed and shook her head. "Nah, he just doesn't look like these dipshits making the dancers work for a couple singles. He hasn't even bought a dance."

"Not for lack of trying. There go Misty's skinny ass."

Chanté peered across the club and frowned at Misty stumbling toward his booth on her skinny legs and even skinnier platform heels. Chanté rolled her eyes and sighed.

"You better go get her before she fuck up your dough," Angie said. "He might not be rich, but he definitely looks like a good tipper."

Chanté agreed. She pushed away from the bar and walked, as quickly as her tall shoes and short legs would allow, to the booth that had somehow become the near-center of her attention since her shift started.

Saraiya's first rule of employee-customer relations at The Petal was that there were none unless money changed hands, and even then, drinks and dances were all that money could buy.

Now, Chanté was no one's fool. She knew that some of the dancers and a few of the waitresses stretched those rules as far as they could go without breaking for a little — or a lot — of extra cash. And if they were hellbent on snapping Saraiya's rules in half, they respected her — or were terrified enough of her — to take that business offsite. No one talked about it, but everyone knew. Everyone also knew that Chanté flirted close to that line, but she hadn't stepped over it. Yet.

She'd thought about it and been propositioned by more than a few customers to give it some very serious consideration, but she'd never taken anyone up on their offer. She hadn't known why and had been too busy with work, school, and her dreams to fully interrogate it. Besides, finding a sugar daddy to ease the transition from ward of the state to independent adult had been Caleb's life-changing fantasy, not Chanté's. If anyone was going to save Chanté, she'd always just assumed it would be herself, not some rich man with a penthouse apartment his wife didn't know about and a bit of a fetish he was too nervous to take home.

But the truth, she realized half an hour ago, was that she'd just never met a man who inspired the kind of reckless abandon necessary to break a few rules. But maybe now she had. And Misty, the worst dancer in the club and resident fire hazard, was in danger of annoying the man Chanté very much wanted to use as her personal stage prop into leaving before she could test that theory.

She watched in horror as Misty plopped into the booth next to HIM with an exhausted, inebriated grin.

Chanté rounded the booth with a bright smile on her face. "Misty!" she squealed. "Saraiya's looking for you." It was a plausible lie. Saraiya was always looking for one or another of the dancers to get on stage, move on from a table that had stopped spending, or take a break. She was the general manager, den mother, and disciplinarian, and if Misty had been in her right mind, she would have hopped to it. But Misty was very rarely in her right mind. Her bleach blonde hair constantly smelled like hairspray and cigarettes, and the rest of her, especially her breath, usually smelled like gin.

Chanté didn't look at him; she was too embarrassed. She focused all of her attention on getting Misty up and as far away from him as possible.

"Tell her I'm workin'," Misty slurred.

"I—"

"It's okay," the customer said easily, casually, as if this kind of inappropriate thing happened regularly.

Chanté turned to him slowly, meeting his eyes hesitantly. "Are you sure?" she asked.

He smiled at her, his full lips tilting and his dark eyelashes batting seductively at her. He tipped his head forward in a single nod.

"Oh. Okay," she whispered.

"She can rest here if she needs to," he said.

Chanté wanted to tell him that, technically, she could not; Saraiya wouldn't like that. If a dancer needed to sit, club policy was to sit on a lap that was paying or backstage, never at the bar, and never in a booth unless money had been exchanged. But that was a lot of company policy for a customer who definitely didn't care.

She bit her lip and turned to look around the room, searching for any sign of Saraiya.

When she turned back to the booth, her customer was reaching into his jacket pocket. He pulled a fifty-dollar bill from his wallet and slid it across the table toward Misty, but his eyes were firmly rooted to Chanté's face. She exhaled in relief, and his smile widened.

"Better?" he asked.

Chanté nodded quickly, smiling shyly at him.

"What kinda dance you want?" Misty asked before falling into a fit of wracking coughs, effectively cutting into whatever moment had passed between Chanté and her customer.

"Maybe you should head to the back?" Chanté asked Misty in a tentative, shaky voice.

"Is that a question or an order?" he asked.

"I'm just a waitress," Chanté hissed. "I don't give commands, especially not to dancers."

"Sounds like a cop-out to me."

"Hey, I'm trying to help here. Do you want my help?"

"If help is all you're offering..."

Chanté's mouth went dry. "What...what else... I—"

Saraiya's voice cut off Chanté's stammers. "That's it. You're done for the night."

Chanté turned just in time to see Saraiya haul Misty up from the booth.

"I was workin'."

"Workin' my nerves, yes. Workin' the bar, absolutely. Making money? No. Get backstage," she hissed under her breath. Chanté didn't know if Saraiya was trying to do this quietly, but it wasn't working. Everyone at the closest booths and tables had turned to watch as Saraiya helped a sulking Misty up from the booth and steadied her as she stood on her heels.

Saraiya turned to Chanté's customer with a friendly, professional smile on her face. "I'm so sorry about this. Chanté'll get you a drink on the house," she said and turned away.

Chanté nodded once and walked quickly to the bar where she ordered another glass of cranberry juice and then focused much harder than necessary on not spilling a drop as she took it back to his booth.

"Here ya go," she said.

"Thank you, Chanté," he murmured, saying her name at a pitch that forced her to lean in as if they were having an intimate conversation and everything that passed his lips was a caress.

People had said her name lots of ways — yelled it like a curse, spat it through their lips like it was poison, somehow mispronounced it as Chantell, laughed around the two syllables with glee — but no one had ever purred it like it was made of silk, something lovingly crafted and expensive. Something cherished.

It made her skin warm and her slit slick and her mouth dry. "Do you want a lap dance?" she blurted out, rubbing her suddenly sweaty hands across the backs of her thighs.

He lifted his eyebrows with keen interest. "Are you allowed to do that?"

Her eyes darted away in shame, and she shook her head.

"If I were your boss, this would probably be a mark in your file or whatever."

"But you're not my boss," she whispered, looking at him again.

She watched as his eyes moved up and down her body. "No, I'm not."

He swung his long legs out of the booth and stepped forward, getting close enough to touch. Close enough to wrap his taller, bigger, leaner body around hers and keep her still or grab her and drag her back into the booth with him. Chanté's mouth fell open on a gasp, imagining that — her ass nestling against the hard mound in his lap, her legs spread around his hips, grinding against him. Getting herself off on him, for him, and getting paid to do it.

He licked his lips and lifted his hand to her face, gently caressing the soft roundness of her left jaw, up to her earlobe, and then down to swipe across her chin.

She looked up at him through her eyelashes, panting softly as he gently petted her.

"Next time I come back," he whispered only loud enough for her to hear. "I want to see you on that stage."

Chanté sucked in a shuddering breath. "Why do you care?"

"Who doesn't want to give a beautiful woman all their money?" he teased.

She rolled her eyes.

His thumb pressed quickly into her bottom lip. "Do you want to dance?" he asked seriously.

"Yes."

"Then I want you to have whatever it is you want."

She shook her head gently. "But why do you care?"

"To be honest, I don't know," he admitted with a smile. His fingers squeezed her chin before his hand fell away. He took a step back, and Chanté shivered slightly at the loss of his warmth. She hadn't realized he was so close and so warm. "Maybe when I see you on stage, we can both get some answers."

She squinted at him as he pulled a wad of bills from his pocket and set them carefully on the table.

She glanced down at those bills and shook her head. "That's a two hundred percent tip," she whispered in awe.

"And you didn't even get naked. Imagine if you did," he said with a wink.

She rolled her eyes but couldn't stop herself from smiling. She watched as he turned and strolled out of the club.

"Fuck. Me," she whispered when he was far enough away not to accidentally hear her words.

"Girl, me too," Angie said, appearing next to her out of nowhere.

___________

four

___________

Chanté slipped back into her tennis shoes and shoved her heels into her bag. She'd already shoved her tips into her bra and picked up Kenny's wings, putting them in the bottom of her backpack so she could keep her hands free just in case. She'd never had a problem, but Saraiya recommended extreme caution after a shift, especially for girls like Chanté who didn't have a car.

"Team meeting, ladies," Saraiya called from the hallway. Chanté, Angie, and the new waitress, whose name Chanté couldn't remember because they'd never spoken in the two shifts they'd worked together, all sighed.

A cacophonous groan sounded from the dancers' locker room, but the waitresses didn't waste any time sympathizing. They grabbed their bags and headed down the hall to Saraiya's office, hoping to snatch up seats before the dancers arrived. Unlike the dancers, the waitresses were used to this kind of after-shift meeting, and they knew that after an entire shift on their feet, the difference between a chair and leaning against a wall could feel like the chasm between heaven and hell.

Chanté practically fell onto a cushion at the end of the pleather couch in Saraiya's office, her backpack resting on her lap and clutched to her chest. She looked at the watch on her wrist and calculated how much time until the next night bus going in her direction. If this was a quick meeting, she could dart across the street to the bus stop under the street light in front of the Lora's liquor store, catch the N15 toward campus, and get off around the corner from her apartment. She could be washing off the glitter body lotion she wore when she worked in half an hour, tops.

If this wasn't a quick meeting, she could go to the same bus stop and wait for the local 152. It would take about twice as long to get to her neighborhood, and she'd have to walk about two blocks farther once she got off the bus, but she could always call Kenny to meet her at her stop if she was nervous or wanted to harass him into giving her a piggyback ride because her feet were too sore.

Options sorted, she relaxed against the couch arm and waited for the meeting to start.

The dancers filed into the office and shoved the newbie waitress out of her chair. Chanté pressed even closer against the arm of the couch and hoped no one noticed her. She had a bit of waitress seniority, but not much, and no waitress outranked any of the dancers. Not even Misty.

Saraiya started the meeting as soon as Pebbles filed into the room and settled onto Kay's lap.

"Alright, let's get started so we can get the hell out of here as quickly as possible." A murmur of tired agreement rippled through the room. "As you know, The Petal has a new owner."

"Oh, you 'bout to finally tell us who you sold out to?" one of the dancers, Eve, challenged.

Saraiya rolled her eyes but otherwise ignored her. "The deal was complicated, but it's been settled. The good news is that the new owner isn't interested in changing the day-to-day operations. The house cuts won't change, and I'll still be in charge of schedules. As far as everyone in this room is concerned, it's business as usual."

"Then why the hell are we having this meeting?" Misty rasped, a cigarette already hanging from her lips.

Saraiya ignored her as well. "The *only* thing that's going to change is that we're losing a VIP room. The new owner wants to have an office here, and the only place we could spare without displacing any of you was the VIP room at the far end of the hall."

"That's it?" one of the dancers asked. Chanté didn't see who.

"That's a big issue, actually," Kay piped up. "On busy nights, the three VIP rooms aren't enough. Not that you'd know that," she shot back.

Kay wasn't normally nice to anyone besides Pebbles, but she usually kept her temper in check. Chanté was nosy and needed to know who'd pushed Kay over the edge of bare professional respect. She followed the direction of Kay's dismissive glare and landed on Joi, one of the new dancers. She'd been hired barely a week ago after Saraiya had poached her from The Trap, one of The Petal's rivals from across town. At The Trap, Joi had been a star on the brink, but not at The Petal. Not yet, at least. Here, she didn't have any seniority, and she hadn't built the kind of loyal fanbase that was willing to follow her from one club to the next.

But Chanté liked Joi a lot.

Joi's shows were colorful and high-energy. Her ass was fat, and she was one of the more versatile dancers at The Petal. Watching Joi dance was like watching an erotic gymnastic meet. Sometimes, Chanté would stand against the bar at the back of the club, hypnotized by the slow, melodic, almost balletic dances where she bared her skin slowly and surely and ended up naked just before the music ended and the lights went out. The entire club would be quietly riveted, a near-unheard of thing at The Petal. Other times, Chanté would be dancing right along with the pumping bass, watching as Joi's ass, hips, thighs, and titties shook on perfect beat. Chanté's heart would pound as she watched Joi climb higher and higher up the pole until she flipped her body upside down and planted the soles of her heels on the ceiling. She'd gasp collectively with the rest of the room when Joi dropped down the pole in the span of a heartbeat. She'd hold her breath and wait to see if the woman stopped herself halfway down for an extra shake or made it all the way to the floor, falling into a perfect split.

As far as Chanté was concerned, everything that happened on stage at The Petal was art, but Joi was a master in the making, and Chanté was mesmerized. She smiled shyly in Joi's direction, but the other woman dropped her head and pressed her lips together.

Kay turned to Saraiya. "What are those of us who actually pull in the ballers supposed to do when there are more than two big wallets in the building?"

Saraiya took a deep breath before turning to Kay. The two women liked each other about as much as Chanté liked her Communications professor, Dr. Wyndemere. Chanté knew why she hated her professor, but she hadn't been able to figure out the beef between these two women in nearly a year.

"Part of the reason the owner wants an office here is that we're considering a full renovation of The Petal. The owner wants to get a feel for the club before making any big decisions. This is an inconvenience, I realize that, but the goal is to make long-term improvements so we can all make more money."

"The Petal gone shut down," the new waitress called out. She sounded scared, and unfortunately, that emotion pricked at everyone's anxiety that this was a possibility, a fear that had been simmering ever since Saraiya announced that she was looking for a buyer or maybe an investor.

Chanté clutched her backpack even tighter to her chest, wincing as a zipper pull bit into the bare skin over her ribcage. She swallowed nervously, forcing herself to release her hold on her bag just a little bit by reminding herself that she could find another job. The problem was that she didn't want another job. Tips at The Petal were great, and Saraiya always took her class schedule into consideration when giving her shifts. But to be honest, she didn't *want* to work anywhere else. She liked waitressing at The Petal just as it was. And she wanted to dance here so badly it was a palpable thing she could feel in her bones.

"The Petal is *not* shutting down," Saraiya said, raising her voice to cut through the anxious murmurs. "I didn't want to have to sell, but we needed someone with the money to do things like replace the furnace, get more security, and maybe even pay for some advertising to get new blood in here. I couldn't do that. But I didn't sell to just anyone, and we are not shutting down," she repeated. "I promise that."

"As do I," someone said, stepping into the room.

Chanté's head tipped back to look up at the tallest woman she'd ever seen. The woman's blonde hair was as pale as her skin, and her suit looked like it cost more than Chanté's tips from the last three months. Maybe four months.

"Perfect timing," Saraiya said, relaxing into a smile.

Chanté was surprised to find Saraiya, who'd thrown fully grown men out of here single-handedly, beaming up at this new woman as if she were a Renaissance painter, waiting to become her muse. Saraiya didn't beam at anyone or anything besides stacks of money at the end of a shift. She found the open admiration on her boss's face unnerving even though she didn't know exactly what was turning her off. So, she kept her mouth shut. Besides, she'd probably looked just like that a few hours ago while watching the dancers on stage or staring into her customer's eyes, silently wishing he would touch her, grab her, hold her.

Either way, Chanté didn't have a leg to stand on, so

she observed the way the rest of the room was reacting to this new addition instead.

"I'm so excited to be meeting you all," the new owner said. "I watched your shows tonight, and you were wonderful. Just wonderful." Chanté watched as this unknown white woman turned in a circle at the center of a room filled primarily with Black and brown women and clapped slowly as if they were circus performers or something.

The scene felt ominous to Chanté, or maybe comical. It definitely didn't sit right with her spirit, at the very least.

"As Saraiya said, I'm not here to change anything negatively. I want to make your lives better, so we can all make so much more money together."

The crowd murmured, and some of the dancers shifted in their seats. Chanté noticed for the first time just how often the group tended to respond in one accord. *Interesting*, she thought to herself.

Just as soon as she had that thought, however, Kay spoke up. "And why should we believe you when you watched us from the side hallway like a peeping Tom and haven't even told us your name?"

Chanté swallowed nervously, her eyes darting around the room. Truth be told, she should have been terrified at this turn of events. As calm as Saraiya and the new owner seemed, Chanté could feel the tension rippling between the three women.

It didn't seem to escape anyone that Kay's outburst could cost them all. The new owner didn't need a reason to fire any of them, and Kay's attitude was as good an excuse as any to decide to clean house. There was nothing stopping her from latching onto the dancer's subordination and running with it.

A part of Chanté's brain was terrified that the new owner would respond in exactly the way she was imagining. But a much larger part of Chanté was too nosy to care about consequences. She bit her lips to stop from smiling, and her eyes darted from one woman to the other to the other. She also mentally accepted that she would be catching the local bus home tonight.

God, she hoped these women made the slower ride home worth it.

They did not.

Their new boss turned slowly to face off with Kay, and the entire room braced itself. Some of the women closest to the confrontation leaned away, and one of the dancers actually scooted her chair out of the direct line of fire. Meanwhile, Chanté leaned forward. The room was completely quiet, even though it was packed to the gills. The silence stretched on for five, ten, fifteen seconds until it was broken by Chanté's soft gasp, that gentle intake of breath full of excited anticipation.

She loved the suspense of it all.

No one turned toward her, though. Why would

they? Who cared about the perverse excitement she was feeling when this head-to-head was brewing?

"You're right," the new owner said, slipping her slim, pale hands into the pockets of her oversized trousers.

The rest of the room seemed to exhale, but not Chanté. That minor acquiescence didn't cut the tension between them, and it certainly didn't erase the nervous fury on Saraiya's face.

"How rude of me," the woman continued. "My name is Mia Malkova. My family and I have a number of real estate holdings throughout the city, most of them on the East Side. But it's been my dream to see the West Side get the same economic attention, and The Petal is the first piece of my new portfolio."

That seemed to dissipate some of the tension, at least for Saraiya. Kay, however, leaned back in her chair — forcing Pebbles to shift her weight to sit more comfortably — and sucked her teeth in annoyance. Mia was unfazed. She continued turning around the room, but this time much more slowly so she could make eye contact with each dancer and waitress in turn.

When her eyes locked with Chanté's for a fraction of a second, the energy of gossipy interest melted away and was replaced by confusion. Her eyes were empty depths of ice blue.

*Huh*, Chanté thought to herself. *Now, that's very interesting. And weird.*

"I won't keep you ladies here any longer, but I wanted to introduce myself to you all and let you know that it's my goal to make The Petal the best strip club in Cleveland. And I want to do it with your help. Get home safe, everyone," she ended with a sharp clap of her hands.

Chanté didn't like that clap. It reminded her of her high school PE teacher, who used to clap condescendingly in the students' faces when he was done speaking to them, whether or not they were done speaking to him. Kay wasn't Chanté's favorite person in the club, but in that moment, Chanté decided that she was on Kay's side — assuming there were sides, of course. But that remained to be seen.

So, for right now, Chanté darted out of Saraiya's office toward the side entrance. She checked her watch as she jogged and swore. She had three minutes to catch the fast bus. That was more than enough time, so long as she didn't dawdle. When she pushed out of the fire exit, she shivered at the cold. She'd have to switch from her jean jacket to something thicker and warmer for her next shift. She jogged down the dark alleyway toward the street.

The Petal was in the middle of the block. Chanté knew from experience that she would waste precious time going to a sidewalk. She stopped at the curb on the mostly silent street and looked left and right. Somewhere, she heard glass breaking and someone yelling out of a window for someone to shut up. There was an old factory down the street where local promoters sometimes threw raves, and Chanté could hear the music thumping in the night air. She looked right again and saw the bright headlights of a bus. She didn't know if it was her bus or not, but she couldn't take the chance. She'd made that mistake before, thinking she had a few more minutes than she did to walk to the end of the block to cross the street legally or even to dip into the Lora's store for a drink and a bag of chips. She'd missed the fast bus more than once being careless, but not tonight.

She looked left and right one more time for any sign of the police cars that often patrolled the area when the bars and clubs were closing, just waiting to fine or arrest someone for the smallest infraction, especially jaywalking, which usually turned into a drunk and disorderly charge.

Chanté didn't see anything that looked like 5-0, so she darted out into the street. She rushed to the other side and up the street to the bus stop. Just before she got there, someone stepped out of the Lora's shop.

Chanté took in his tall frame in an instant, which was easy to do because she'd spent nearly an hour watching him out of the corner of her eyes. His hair was longer than she'd expected now that he'd set it free from the bun at the crown of his head. If he was interested in constructive feedback, she already had a paragraph composed in her head about what his dark, glossy, wavy hair falling over his shoulders did to her panties. What he had likely done to lots of people.

His brown skin looked rich and vibrant, even under the cheap fluorescent light spilling onto the sidewalk between them.

He turned to her, and the smile that split his face made her come to a hard stop.

Chanté's heart was pounding, her chest heaving, her mouth dry.

"Long shift?" the customer from the back booth asked, walking slowly toward her.

She nodded.

"That your bus?"

She nodded again, even though she wasn't one hundred percent certain that was correct.

He moved toward the curb and stood leisurely next to the bus stop.

Chanté stepped to the left, standing at the curb, but not getting closer to him… Well, not much closer.

"Water?" he asked, holding a plastic bottle toward her. She moved forward and grabbed it at the neck.

"Thanks," she whispered.

He nodded and reached into his pocket. "Granola bar?" he asked with a bright lift in his tone that made the deep rumble of his voice seem playful. But there was something about playful on a man like him that also seemed dangerous, Chanté thought, although she hadn't ever met a man like him, so what did she know?

He extended his left arm toward her. Her stomach rumbled and mixed with the sound of the bus behind her. Chanté reached for the snack and grasped it with the tips of her fingers.

He didn't let go. Instead, he tugged gently at the bar, and for some reason, Chanté didn't let go either. She let him pull her closer.

"What are you still doing around here?" she asked. "You left the club hours ago."

The left side of his mouth lifted into the sexiest lopsided grin she'd ever seen. He let the granola bar go. The bus pulled along the curb beside them.

The bus doors opened, and the warm air from inside spilled out around them.

"Come on, Chanté," Miss Francine called.

The man smiled at her.

She shivered and nodded, turning on suddenly weak legs.

"See you next time, Chanté," he called just as the doors began to close.

"Who was that?" Miss Francine asked.

Chanté smiled but didn't speak. She didn't think she could form a coherent sentence, let alone explain that that man was the man she was going to marry or fuck until she passed out from dehydration. Maybe both. God, she hoped it was both.

She fumbled inside her bag for her bus pass and showed it to Miss Francine, more as a formality than anything. The bus pulled into the street, and Chanté walked toward the back of the bus. A figure on the sidewalk caught her attention. She turned to see him watching her, smiling as Miss Francine hummed approvingly.

five

ONE MONTH LATER

The worst part about working at The Petal once the weather cooled was changing for her shift. She went from bundled up to as close to naked as the waitresses were allowed to get in practically a heartbeat, and it was disorienting.

Last winter, Chanté's first winter waitressing at The Petal, had been an adventure; she never knew if the heat was going to be working or not. She also didn't know if it was the faulty furnace that would make the club feel like the inside of a meat locker or because Saraiya was behind on the utility bills, but she learned very quickly that no one talked about The Petal's money problems. Well, *everyone* talked about the club's money problems, including some of their regulars, but never in front of Saraiya.

When she'd announced that she was looking to sell

the club, everyone had been shocked and confused. No one knew what to expect, but Chanté was pleasantly surprised at the noticeable change in temperature when Stevie let her in the club.

"It's warm," she exclaimed.

"Mmmhm. The new owner had somebody come put in a new furnace last week while we were closed," Stevie said in a disgruntled voice.

"That's a good thing," Chanté called over her shoulder.

"We'll see about that."

In the locker room, Chanté switched from her Chuck Taylors into her platform heel boots. She was wearing her signature miniscule jean shorts and crop top. She'd covered her top half with a plain black sweatshirt and a puff coat and tugged on a pair of bright pink tights under her shorts to match her top.

She closed her locker, snapped the lock in place, and headed to the floor.

The door to the dancers' dressing room was closed, and Chanté frowned slightly.

"Long time, no see," Angie said as soon as Chanté walked out onto the floor.

"Midterms," Chanté breathed.

Angie nodded. She'd dropped out of college after her first year after realizing that she hated it. She was waitressing at The Petal to pay for her cosmetology classes, and sometimes she offered Chanté a haircut or manicure when she had a test coming up. Chanté always accepted.

"How'd they go?" Angie asked.

Chanté shrugged. "Engineering and Program Design went great. Sociology is up in the air. Completely bombed my English essay, though."

"How you fuck up an essay? All you do is talk?" Angie teased.

Chanté pushed her lightly and rolled her eyes. "Shut up. Hey, Saraiya."

"Welcome back, Little Miss Studious," her boss teased.

"Thanks for giving me the week off."

Saraiya smiled but never looked up from the clip-board in her hands. "Any time. We're going to need a website upgrade soon enough. As long as you're prepared to say yes, we're good."

"Yes, ma'am."

"Yes, ma'am," Angie teased in a high-pitched voice that didn't sound anything like Chanté's.

"Don't you have drinks to deliver?" Saraiya warned.

"Yes, ma'am," Angie sassed with a smile. She loaded up her tray and strolled away with a laugh.

"You too," Saraiya said to Chanté. "Booths."

Chanté nodded and waved at the bartenders as she passed. She weaved her way through the tables, looking left and right, taking in the crowd. Sometimes, she could make a reliable estimation of her potential tips by taking a vibe check of the room when she came on shift. She wasn't always one hundred percent accurate, but she got near enough to amuse herself when the crowd was thin and to keep pushing when she barely had a moment to breathe, let alone sit down for a few minutes.

She was a few steps from the booths when she felt it — a solid weight in her stomach and electricity crackling over her skin. He was back, and he'd spotted her; it was his gaze on her that made her hot and bothered. She almost wished she'd worn less clothing. No, she wished she was wearing a few more layers, just so she could take them off. Slowly. For him. The hair on her arms was standing on end, her throat had dried out, and worst — or best — of all, her nipples had tightened almost painfully into hard points.

When she rounded along the back booth — the same booth where he'd sat last time — she let out a soft, gasping breath. "You're back," she whispered.

He was reclined in his seat, in a casual sprawl. He smiled up at her as if he'd been waiting for her. The small romantic part of Chanté's brain that wanted to taste this man spilling across her tongue decided that she would let herself believe that he had, actually, been waiting for her.

"I told you I'd be back," he said.

"That was a month ago," she challenged.

He sucked his bottom lip into his mouth, and Chanté watched, enraptured, as his perfectly white, straight, even teeth bit into his smooth brown bottom lip.

"Have you been waiting for me, Chanté?"

She swallowed, still staring at his mouth. If she'd wanted to pretend as if she hadn't been waiting for him to come back since that first night, she'd flubbed it big time without even thinking. Chanté was good at pretending, but she found herself not wanting to pretend in front of him. She had been waiting for him. Every bus trip across town, she'd struggled to read her textbook or chat with Miss Francine or even listen to music because she'd been preoccupied, wondering if tonight would be the night when he showed up again. During her week off for midterms, she'd been thankful for the break while also terrified that he would pop back up on a night when she wasn't working. She'd even had a nightmare that while she was practically living in the library, he was sitting in this booth being tall, dark, and handsome, ordering his cranberry juice from someone who wasn't her. She'd imagined him getting a lap dance from someone who wasn't her. She'd woken up in a cold sweat, feeling ridiculous but still vaguely angry. And then she'd been horny, so she'd pulled a vibrator from her dresser and fucked herself back to sleep. It was a very weird week away from work.

But now, here he was, smiling at her like a horny Cheshire cat, asking if she'd been waiting for him. She rolled her eyes and put her right hand on her hip. "Obviously."

His eyes darted to the stage behind her and then back to her face. "Is there something you want to show me?"

Chanté deflated sadly. She shook her head and frowned.

He sighed softly; she thought that breath was full of disappointment.

"What are you waiting for?" he asked gently.

Chanté wished he had been a little less gentle; she knew how to handle asshole customers, not ones who seemed to care. "This is only your second time here, bro. Don't rush me," she burst out.

"Bro?" he laughed.

"Don't judge me, either."

His face sobered. "I'd never."

The earnestness in his voice shocked her into silence.

"I just hate to see someone with all your enthusiasm waste it."

"I'm not wasting anything. I have time."

He shrugged. "Time. You're, at the very least, wasting time. That could be you up there right now, you know? You could be making far more doing that than bringing assholes like me drinks. That could be you."

Chanté knew he was right, and she didn't like it. Nor did she want to confront it, so she turned toward the stage just as Joi sauntered on in a full mesh bodysuit.

Chanté's lips parted in surprise. She'd never seen this outfit before. She smiled briefly as one of her favorite songs to study to, "Outlines" by AlunaGeorge, started playing, and Joi began to wrap her body sensuously around the pole. "Joi's one of a kind," she said.

She was so wrapped up in watching the performance that she didn't notice him stand from the booth. "You're one of a kind," he whispered into her ear. "But it's nice to know what you like."

She turned slowly and came face to face with him for the first time in a month. A very long month. He was closer than he'd ever been before, and up close, he seemed even more dangerous. Up close, his hair seemed darker and looked silkier, his cologne was soft but spicy and filled her nostrils, he seemed taller and broader, and his smile made her panties wetter than a month ago.

"And what do you plan to do with that kind of information?" she asked in a rough whisper.

He stared down at her with purpose, and she stared back with what she hoped was naked longing because she very much wanted to get naked with him.

And then he backed away. He reached into his pocket and pulled out a small but respectable wad of bills in a money clip. Very tacky. She loved it.

Chanté watched as he peeled two fifty-dollar bills from the stack and then moved to slip the money under her shirt into the side of her halter bra. Her mouth fell open in a shocked smile as one of his fingers brushed her hard, sensitive nipple. She tried to swallow the moan that bubbled up in her throat, but she couldn't; it fell from her lips like a bomb, obliterating every other sound in the room as far as Chanté was concerned.

Suddenly, there was only him.

"What's your name?" she breathed. The wrong response per club policy, but the right response for the gentle pulsing of blood rushing to her clit.

This time, when his thumb brushed her nipple, it wasn't an accident, assuming that the first touch had been. "I'll tell you next time I see you," he said and then turned away with a devastating smile on his face.

"Fuck," Chanté breathed to herself.

"Double fuck," Angie echoed beside her.

THE PROBLEM with starting the shift with an unfortunately figurative bang was that everything after paled in comparison. None of her customers were as fine or generous in their tipping as him. None of the music made her heart race as fast as it had when he'd leaned close, and she'd been enveloped in the scent of him. Even catching a mid-shift encore of Joi's new routine when the crowd had changed or was drunk enough to experience it as if it was the first time all over again didn't pull Chanté out of the rut she'd been in since he'd left.

Her disappointment wasn't just frustrating; it was expensive. By the time her shift was over, the wad of cash in her bra from her tips was much less than normal. She'd felt too hungover after that brief encounter to put on the mask she needed to charm her customers into sparing a few singles for her fully clothed when there were dancers, in much less, actually trying to get their attention. Being a waitress in a strip club was a battle on the best of nights; it felt like a war tonight.

Chanté changed back into her tennis shoes with a relieved sigh at the end of the night.

"You alright?" Saraiya asked, standing in the doorway.

"Yeah. Just still a little tired from exams," Chanté lied. She smiled quickly at Saraiya the way she hadn't been able to smile at her customers all night, but she didn't stop moving. She didn't want to miss her bus, and she definitely didn't want to give Saraiya any chance to interrogate her further.

"Well, go home and get some real sleep. The

Saturday crowd won't take kindly to a lackluster performance on or offstage."

Chanté zipped up her backpack and nodded. "Yes, ma'am."

Saraiya backed into the hallway so Chanté could walk past her.

"See you tomorrow," Chanté said, shoving her bag onto her back.

"See you tomorrow. Hey, Chanté!" Saraiya called.

Chanté turned and forced herself not to smile any harder or wider. She couldn't give herself away like that.

"Did you see the notice?" Saraiya asked, throwing Chanté for a loop.

"N-notice?"

"We're having tryouts for new dancers next week."

Chanté's mouth went dry, and her stomach clenched, but not in the good way. She was terrified. "I-I…" Chanté's voice trailed off. She was sweating, and not because of the new furnace.

"No pressure," Saraiya said. "But if you're interested, all you have to do is sign up."

"Are you still going to be the one choosing, or… I mean, is the new owner?"

"We'll both choose," Saraiya said, "but you know I'll always be pulling for you."

Chanté's cheeks burned.

"Now get out of here before Miss Francine comes to yell at me about you missing your bus."

Chanté nodded and waved before darting from the club's side door. She speed-walked toward the mouth of the alleyway. She was almost at the sidewalk when a figure moved into her line of sight. Chanté froze on the spot, cursing under her breath. She was supposed to keep her key ring in hand, with her rape whistle and the military-grade pepper spray Kenny had gotten her at the ready. Sometimes she forgot, and for a brief second, she thought she'd pay the ultimate price for this lapse in preparation, but then the figure moved to stand under a streetlight. Chanté knew who he was by then, and she started walking again as if he was pulling her into his orbit.

Not that he needed to pull her; she was the definition of ready and willing.

"How was your shift?" he asked when she was close.

"You shouldn't be back here."

"I agree. This place needs better security. A light, at least. I don't like the idea of you running around a dark alleyway after work."

"I can take care of myself," she said defensively.

"I bet you can," he chuckled.

She scowled up at him, but her heart wasn't in it at all.

"Let's go," he said, tipping his head down the street, *away* from her bus stop.

"I'm not going anywhere with you," she said, even though there was a small, tiny, hardly noticeable part of her brain screaming that she should go with him N O W, anywhere he wanted.

"I just want to walk you to the bus stop," he said.

"Bus stop's that way," she said.

"Sidewalk's that way," he added. "And I just happen to be walking across the street to the liquor store for a snack. Would you like to walk together?"

"Why?" She crossed her arms in front of her chest and cocked her left hip out with just a little bit of attitude.

"I'm trying to be chivalrous. That means—"

"I know what it means, and I know you're bullshitting me right now."

"I like you," he breathed in a shocked whisper.

"I'm likeable," she said. "Answer my question."

He smiled down at her and checked the time on his left wrist. "I just did. How about dinner? Did you eat dinner at work?"

"No."

"Well, let me buy you dinner, and I'll get you back here in time for the next night bus."

"A bottle of water and a granola bar? I'm good."

"You ate that granola bar," he said confidently.

"Just 'cause I ate it don't mean I want another. I have granola bars at home."

He rolled his eyes at her. "Well, if you hurry up and choose, I'll buy you something else."

Chanté's eyes lit up at those words, her favorite words, as it happened. *I'll buy you something.*

When she'd gotten into college, she'd applied for every scholarship and grant she was eligible for, and a few she wasn't to minimize the amount of student loans she'd have to take out. Because of that, she'd managed to cobble together an aid package and enough hours at The Petal to pay for her classes and books — within reason — rent and utility bills, but food was always an issue.

Some months, she could finagle the perfect amount of discounted appetizers at The Petal, sandwiches, and snacks she carried around in her backpack to her classes, and the very occasional takeout meal, usually shared with Kenny — who always managed to pay for more than his share if not the whole meal — to make ends meet. Still, the end of the month and between semesters were the hardest times, and today was the twenty-eighth of the month. Add onto that she'd missed an entire week of wages and tips. Someone offering to buy her a meal might as well have been a proposal for marriage.

So yeah, she'd eaten the granola bar he'd given her a month ago, and she was going to take him up on his offer to buy dinner tonight. "There's a burger joint around the corner," she said casually.

"SOUNDS GOOD TO ME."

"And just to clarify, you are paying, right?"

His laughter echoed in the alleyway. "You've got some balls."

"Big hairy ones," she said. "Please respond."

"Of course, I'm paying, Chanté."

"Good. Night bus comes through every fifty-five minutes," she added, just to clarify.

His eyes found hers in the dark, and he nodded. "I'll have you at your bus stop in plenty of time. I promise."

She uncrossed her arms and smiled, bouncing up onto the balls of her feet. "Great."

"This'll be the fastest date of my life."

"This isn't a date. I don't date."

"What does that mean?"

"Exactly what I said."

"You're in the prime of your life," he said.

"You sound old. Are you old?"

"I'm just saying that you're in college. You should be dating."

"I don't have time to date," she said, having been over this with Caleb more than a few times. Thankfully, she never had to retread this topic with Kenny since he was as committed to his schoolwork as she was. "I go to school. I work. I sleep. I study. I don't date."

"Maybe you just haven't met the right person," he said.

She tipped her head back and smiled up at him as she reached for his left wrist. Her fingers dipped under his long-sleeved sweater, which felt soft, like cashmere, maybe, but his downy hair was even softer. When her fingers brushed against his skin, she sucked in a sharp breath. It was colder outside than when she'd arrived, but touching his skin made Chanté hot like they were standing on this street in the middle of a summer day.

"Maybe," she whispered.

"We should go," he said in a gruff whisper that sounded strained to her ears.

Chanté brushed two fingers over the clasp of his watch. It wouldn't take much effort to unclasp it and slip it into her pocket before he noticed. She could do that and tell him she'd changed her mind and then be nestled into a seat on her way home long before he even knew it was gone. She could swing by a connect she had in the student-athlete dorms and have the watch pawned before her first class tomorrow morning. She hadn't had to resort to pickpocketing again since enrolling in college, but she didn't want to let that talent slip away. She never knew when she'd need it again.

She didn't rob him, though. Her lips parted on soft breaths, and he blinked back at her, his eyes focused on her mouth. Her heart was hammering a rhythmic melody against her chest. She left his watch in place and smoothed those two fingers down across his palm, her touch lingering on his hand the way his eyes lingered on her lips.

"I'm gonna need to get something for my roommate, too," she said and turned away, heading toward the burger joint around the corner.

Knowing he would follow.

six

"Great job," Smith said into Asif's ear.

Asif winced and wished he'd tried even harder to leave his two-way receiver behind so he could be in the field without the other man in his ear. Although, the problem wasn't actually that he was in the field and Smith's voice was annoying; it was that he didn't like the intrusion on his time with Chanté.

He'd been waiting a month to see her again.

"Hurry up, I'm hungry," she said, smiling as she wrapped her arms around one of his and pulled him forward.

"Oh, you've got her right where you want her," Smith said like they were bros.

He swallowed the wave of disgust and tried to remind himself of Smith's strengths because Smith was good at some things. The problem, so far as Asif could tell, was that fieldwork was not his strong suit, and he fundamentally didn't understand the amount of energy it took to hold a cover under regular circumstances, let alone when someone like Chanté was bumping into him, trying to feel with the back of one of her hands where his wallet was tucked away.

God, she was wonderful.

Asif wanted to take his earbud out again, but the regional chief blew two gaskets when he found out that Asif had done that during his last visit to The Petal. He wasn't interested in that kind of debrief again, at least for a little while, so he left his receiver in and used every ounce of spare energy he had to shut out the sound of Smith chewing. He thought it would be harder, but actually, it wasn't.

"You're shorter," he said out of the blue after they'd walked half a block down the street.

"Shorter than you? Duh."

"Shorter than you are in the club," he clarified.

"Higher the heels, better the tip," she squeaked, bouncing up onto the balls of her feet with excitement. Fuck.

Asif swallowed at the soft jiggle of her tits under her sweatshirt. "Is that what they say?"

"Who's they?" she asked and then shrugged. "That's what I say after months of very scientific research. I need at least a three-inch heel and a bit of platform to get a good take-home on a weeknight."

"And on the weekends?"

She turned to him, and she was nothing but a big, beautiful smile, baby face, round cheeks, and deep brown eyes. "Four-inch for a decent take, five or higher for something that might change my monthly savings goals or even my life."

"How high were your shoes when we met?"

Her mouth curved into a small smile. "Six inches," she purred up at him.

Asif managed a labored swallow before Smith ruined the moment, for Asif at least, by coughing loudly.

"Jesus," Smith groaned.

Asif managed to keep his eyes on Chanté's face even though he wanted to roll them at the other man, so hard. "I wonder how much more could you make on stage with shoes that high?"

She frowned and rolled her eyes. "Shut up," she muttered.

Asif laughed, a genuine laugh that had nothing to do with the mission or his objective tonight. Chanté made Asif laugh.

"When are you going to audition?"

"When are you going to shut up like I told you?"

"Probably the same day."

The sharp whine that slipped out of her mouth was nearly as adorable as her face. "I'm going to," she whispered.

"When?"

They rounded the corner, but Chanté came to an abrupt stop. She turned and glared up at him. There was nearly a foot separating their faces, but Asif imagined that under the right circumstances, she would be very intimidating.

"What'll you give me if I do?" she asked.

Asif spluttered and smiled. "I seem to remember promising you all the money in my pockets and more. What else do you need?"

"That's after. What are you going to give me now?"

"I don't think that's how this relationship is supposed to go," Asif said.

Chanté sauntered close and batted her long eyelashes at him. "People spend too much time worrying about fitting into boxes. Our relationship can be whatever we want."

Asif's gaze moved up and down Chanté's face, studying her. She looked like exactly what he knew she was, a college student with one hundred dollars in her checking account and just over nine hundred in her savings, ambitious, but maybe a little in over her head. She was taking a full load of classes and didn't have lower than a ninety-four percent in any of them. She waitressed at The Petal at least three days a week, where she wasn't the most popular waitress, but she made good money if her regular deposits into her savings account were any indication.

Asif reminded himself that her life was fragile, and he needed to keep his distance. The closer he got, the more likely he was to fuck up the future she was building for herself. And besides the fact that he didn't have the right to intervene in her life this way, it was Agency policy to make as little of a mess of civilian lives as possible.

Still… "I like the way you think," he said.

Her answering smile was lascivious, and he felt it in his bones. He felt *her* burrowing under his skin. He didn't need to consult The Agency's civilian handbook to see the red flags all around this situation.

"What's your proposition?" he asked in a hoarse voice.

"You could be my patron?"

"Sugar daddy?"

"Patron."

"What's the difference?"

"Sugar daddies usually want sex."

"Not true," Asif said, nudging her with his hip. They didn't have much time tonight, or at all. "There are lots of different kinds of sugar relationships."

"Is that right?" she asked, winking at him.

"It's just fact, not my experience. Besides, you said we could have whatever kind of relationship we want. What we call it doesn't really matter, right?"

She sucked her bottom lip into her mouth and considered. He let her, using the break in their banter to get himself back on track so he could get this mission on solid ground.

When they reached the front of The Yolk, Asif stepped in front of her and reached toward the front door handle. Before he could pull it open, Chanté grabbed his forearm. When he turned to her, she had a serious look on her face.

"I like *patron,*" she said.

"Then we'll call it that," he answered without hesitation. He couldn't give her much, but this, he could give her, even if it meant nothing.

"CHICKEN BURGER," Chanté said with a slow nod. "Good choice."

He smiled at her as their waitress left with their orders written on her pad and their menus tucked underneath her armpit.

Chanté liked The Yolk; it was the best dive diner in the city. The Yolk was best enjoyed between the hours of eleven in the evening and five-thirty in the morning, which was Chanté's favorite time of any day anyway. And a burger and fries at The Yolk didn't cost more than six dollars, which Chanté could usually afford in a pinch.

"I'm happy you approve," he said, leaning back in his seat and watching her.

Chanté squinted at him, enjoying the way his eyebrows drew her eyes to his, and then those dark brown pools sucked her in. "So, about our arrangement," Chanté said. "Let's talk specifics."

"I'm listening."

"Are we talking sex or just dancing?"

He spluttered, and their waitress's hands froze, the large red plastic cups of water hovering just above the table between them.

Chanté turned to look up at the older white woman. Her long gray hair was piled messily into her hairnet under a dingy pink and white tri-fold cap. Chanté smiled at her, but not the kind of smile she used on her own customers. The smile on Chanté's face was politely feral, like her. She'd perfected it as a kid while waiting for one of her parents to pick her up after school, using it to ward off the judgmental yet worried looks of her teachers or to keep people away from her and Caleb's favorite table at the local library, where they spent their days away from the group home. She smiled at the waitress as if to say, "Mind your business, but thank you so much for the water."

The waitress raised her eyebrows and finally set the cups down before turning and walking briskly away.

"Tip her good," Chanté said to… "Also, what the fuck is your name?"

"Talking to you is like being on a rollercoaster. Can we slow down?"

Chanté opened her mouth on a suggestive retort but then snapped her lips together with a mischievous smile.

"I'm not sure if I should ask you what you're thinking right now or not," he whispered.

She shook her head quickly. "It'll make the roller-coaster worse. Let's stay on track. What's your name?"

He watched her for a few seconds as if he was thinking of asking her anyway. Or maybe he was thinking about lying about his name. "Asif," he finally whispered.

Chanté tipped her head to the left and considered him, watching him while he watched her. "Asif," she whispered slowly, tasting his name carefully. His eyes dipped. She poked the tip of her tongue out of the corner of her mouth and then swiped a slow path between her lips to the other corner, just to see if he would follow the movement.

He did. His gaze lingered, devouring the sight. Chanté wanted his mouth to linger over her body and devour her in much the same way his gaze was right now, and then she wanted to return the favor.

"What does it mean?"

"Strong," he whispered, his voice hoarse and his eyes still watching her mouth as if he was waiting for her tongue to reappear. "And yours?"

Chanté frowned and broke the tension between them. She turned to look out the window onto the dark street. A bus passed. It wasn't hers, but that stomach drop moment she felt when she missed a bus gripped her for half a second. Actually, it was a bit like a roller-coaster now that Asif had put that image in her head. "My name means song or sing or something. It's French."

"It's beautiful."

"I know," she said with a smirk, "but like everything my parents ever did, the beauty was incidental. Accidental, even. My dad wanted to name me something like Tiffany."

"You don't seem like a Tiffany," he laughed, drawing her eyes back to him.

"They considered Mariah and Lashaun and Kenesha and Susan." She rolled her eyes with a small smile. "They couldn't decide. They just kept fighting about what to name me for months."

"But they ended up with Chanté?" Asif reminded her gently.

"They named me after the nurse, thank god. She was nice to them, and they liked her more than they liked each other during the delivery. Or ever, probably."

"That's a cute story."

"Is it? I always thought of it as dysfunctional. They were dysfunctional."

"Maybe it can be both," he offered.

Chanté shrugged outwardly, but inwardly, she

tucked that possibility away for consideration later when she was alone. "Were your parents dysfunctional or like normal? You look like they were normal."

Asif ripped open the paper covering of his straw and threw the plastic into his cup. "Define normal," he said before taking a sip.

Chanté wasn't really the type to get distracted by a man's lips moving over a straw, and yet, apparently, that was because she'd never seen Asif sipping water before. She lost track of time for a second, and he let her. He didn't rush her or stop sipping. He gave her plenty of sexy mouth material to tuck away for future consideration as well.

When she'd looked enough to have memorized the adorable dimple on his right cheek, she picked the thread of their conversation back up. "Two parents at home, dinner at the dining room table. Maybe even bedtime stories," she said, still watching his mouth.

He set his cup on the table and licked his lips. She licked her own in unconscious sympathy. Or hunger. One of the two.

"Then no," he said.

Her eyes lifted to his.

"Really?"

"Really. My mother traveled a lot for work. My dad let me eat dinner in front of the tv. I do love a good bedtime story, though," he said, and then his mouth curved into a smile that pulled a smile onto her mouth as well.

They smiled at one another across the table, and Chanté felt the way she had the first time they met — as if the loud room around them and everyone in it had disappeared. "Sex or dancing?" she asked again.

He licked his lips and smiled. "Let's play it by ear and start with dancing. *Practice* dancing," he said. "The goal is to get you on that stage."

"Why? Wouldn't it be great if you had me all to yourself?"

"I'm not territorial," he said. "And you don't strike me as the kind of woman who would like to be kept."

"Define kept."

Asif shook his head. "It's not on the table. Do you have a timeline?" he asked.

"For the sex?"

"For your audition," he corrected, feigning exasperation.

"Oh. Yeah, I guess I do." She picked up her cup and took a sip.

"Do you want to share with the class?" he asked.

"Apparently, there are auditions for new dancers coming soon."

"How soon?"

"Next week," she mumbled under her breath.

Asif shifted forward. "I'm sorry, can you say that a little louder?"

Chanté rolled her eyes and sighed. "I said the auditions are next week."

Asif's face lit up, and he looked sexy as fuck. Chanté resented him but also wanted to sit on that happy face.

"You don't have to look so excited."

"Yes, I do. We have to get to work," he said.

"We?"

"*We*," he echoed. "As your patron, I really am going to have to insist that—"

"No," she cut him off. "That's not how this relationship works."

"I thought we were negotiating that," he teased.

"We are. I just don't like the path we're taking."

Asif threw his head back and burst into laughter. She bit her lips shut, trying not to smile at how happy he looked or feel too smug that she'd caused that.

He finally stopped laughing when their food arrived.

"Thank you," Chanté said to the waitress. The older woman lifted her eyebrows as if shocked that a hussy like her had manners.

"So, if I'm following our negotiations correctly," Asif said as the woman walked away, "the patronage you're proposing is that I give you all my money, and you give me…?"

"The pleasure of knowing you're making my bank

account happy," Chanté replied in a chipper voice. "And a lap dance or two."

Asif squinted across the table as her. "Two minutes ago, there was sex on the table."

"Two minutes ago, you told me we should play that by ear. So now there's just your money, my happiness, and pole dancing."

Asif's smile and eyes softened, and he nodded. "Sounds like a plan. Eat up. I don't want you missing your bus."

Chanté's smile hurt; it was so wide. She shoved two fries in her mouth to hide it.

---

"SO, WHEN DO WE START?" Asif asked.

They'd eaten their food quickly and quietly, almost as if they were comfortable with one another, which they weren't. Not really. But Asif wanted them to be. He knew that they couldn't, though, so he ate quickly, if only because he had a sinking feeling that the more time he spent in Chanté's presence, the more he would want to stay there. The less he would really care about gathering the information he needed on Mia Malkova, even though the Malkovas were terrible people.

But still, he wasn't in a rush to drop Chanté off at her bus stop. He was even dreading the fast-approaching moment of their separation.

"You're eager," she said.

"Why wouldn't I be? You're going to dance for me and rob me? I'm honored."

"Please lower your voice. The police like to stitch people up for bullshit around here," she hissed.

"Oh, I'm sorry. It's consensual robbery," he said too loud.

"Oh my god," she groaned.

They made eye contact. Normally, Asif put a lot of effort into keeping his feelings and thoughts from broadcasting in his eyes, but he didn't do that with Chanté — not tonight and maybe not the night they'd met, a mistake he knew he'd make again.

"We should talk money for real," she ground out.

"I thought we had. You want it all," Asif teased. They'd arrived at the bus stop, and Chanté turned toward him, pressing herself against the bus stop pole.

"How much per dance?" she asked.

"I believe you're supposed to tell me that."

She bit her lip and frowned. She looked nervous, and he thought that was adorable. "H-how much do you think I'm worth?"

Asif frowned at the question. He wanted to tell Chanté to never ask a man that question again. She should never ask anyone to decide her worth, but his heart was pounding hard against his chest with some-thing like righteous indignation. Why didn't Chanté know that already?

He took a step forward.

Chanté braced herself against the pole. She sucked in a breath and held it.

Asif lifted his hand and smoothed his thumb lightly across her hairline. She didn't tilt her head back, but when he looked down at her, he found her peeking up at him through her eyelashes. His hand moved down the side of her face, across her jaw, and under her chin. Gently, he tilted her head back until their eyes met again.

"Everything," he told her. "I think you're worth everything."

The small squeak that escaped from her lips made every muscle in Asif's body tense with need.

"Two hundred dollars a dance," she said.

"Deal."

"My bus is coming," she whispered.

"Give me your phone," he said.

For the first time since they'd met, she didn't fight him. She pulled her phone from her coat pocket and handed it over, watching him as he typed his name and phone number into her contacts.

When he handed it back, she looked up at him with big, dark but bright eyes that pulled him in, and he sunk into her gaze willingly, happily, completely.

The bus pulled up to the curb next to them far too soon for his liking. It wasn't just that Asif wanted to spend just a few more minutes with Chanté, teasing out the tendrils of their attraction, learning the contours of her surprisingly forward yet shy smile.

"Whenever you're ready to start," he whispered.

She nodded her head slowly.

"Have a good night, Chanté."

"You too, Asif."

He stayed on the curb as she boarded and waved at her through the window. He watched until the bus pulled away and the night around him rushed back in, along with Smith's voice.

"Do you have approval to give her that kind of money?" Smith asked.

Asif sighed and turned away from the curb. He walked toward a dark alley across the street from The Petal, where Smith's surveillance van was parked. "You know I don't."

He could hear Smith's nerves in his loud gulp and shaky voice. "Shouldn't we have gotten approval before you made the arrangement?"

"Maybe next time," Asif said, slipping into Smith's van, already pulling his earpiece out and ripping the power source from his back.

"Wh-what do we say when they ask about the expense?"

Asif turned to Smith and tried not to frown. He wanted to. He also wanted to request a new partner, but he knew the optics of that would be terrible. Hell, his career was just starting, and the optics of his presence at The Agency were already compromised. And even though he said he didn't care what anyone thought about him, he did. He cared a lot, maybe too much, to be honest. But he wasn't senior enough to really *not* care. Besides, considering how many people thought he'd only gotten into The Agency because of his connections, he couldn't afford to give the gossip mill any more reason to doubt him. He knew better than most that whatever he did or didn't do wouldn't matter, not really, but he still had a reputation to build and another to protect.

"If anyone asks you about the expenses," Asif said, "send them to me."

Smith nodded eagerly, relaxing for a second before tensing again. "And what are you going to tell them?"

Asif didn't know, and he was too tired to worry about that right now. Besides, he always thought best on his feet. "Get this equipment back to the warehouse. I'll contact you tomorrow evening." And with that, Asif stood from Smith's van. He walked casually from the alleyway to The Petal's parking lot, where he'd parked his car.

On the drive home, he tried to focus his mind back on the mission.

Mia Malkova was Asif's target, but the operation was bigger than her.

The Malkova family was the local head of an international human trafficking ring. A few Agency teams had been tracking the various parts of the global web until they'd landed on the Malkovas as a possible weak link. Asif had identified Mia as the best target after trailing the only daughter of the kingpin across the city, learning her habits. When she'd purchased The Petal, he'd seen his opening. She had real estate all over town, but The Petal was the only property she owned on her own, without one of her brothers or her father. Like everyone else in her family, Mia had a bad habit of mixing business with pleasure. Buying The Petal was like purchasing her own toy box, and considering her ties to human trafficking, the club was as likely to become a future stop in her family's illicit trade in human beings as their other holdings. But the real opening was the rumor that she'd been embezzling from her father and plotting a takeover.

Asif hadn't found any clear evidence that she was, but he didn't need that evidence, nor did he actually care one way or the other. All Asif needed was the opening, and Chanté was the wedge he planned to use to crack the door to Mia Malkova wide open. So to speak.

But first, he needed to get into Mia's new office at The Petal, which was much harder than it should have been.

Mia didn't let anyone get close enough to her without numerous background checks, and unlike her brothers, she destroyed any unsolicited packages she received without even opening them. Mia was only a weak link because she was like her father, too ambitious and treacherous for her own good. If she hadn't been trying to make a move for more power, either in the family business or on her own, The Agency wouldn't have been able to even get close to her, which meant that their window to make this work was only cracked and closing quickly. Once she settled into a routine at The Petal, she'd be near untouchable all over again.

Asif had thought he could simply break into The Petal while it was closed and plant the bug manually, but the first thing Mia did when she acquired the club was put in a state-of-the-art security system. The Agency's tech team had already told them it would take days to hack into the system. They'd gotten to work, but apparently, these things took time.

In the meantime, Asif had suggested explosives to knock the system out or force a hard reset or something.

He was sent back to the drawing board instead.

Chanté's soft cherubic face and thick thighs were Asif's plans b and c, and the plan was shockingly straightforward. Asif already had a rapport with Chanté. All he had to do was exploit their friendly banter and use her to get usable information about The Petal's operations so he could find another way into Mia's new office. He was putting a lot of faith in a part-time waitress, full-time student, and his superiors thought it was a long shot, but Asif had faith in Chanté. As far as Asif was concerned, all roads led to Chanté. Unfortunately, that had very little to do with the mission.

When he walked into the sterile industrial loft assigned to his cover identity, he stripped naked, crawled into bed, remembered Chanté trying not to smile at him across the table at The Yolk while he stroked himself to an orgasm and then fell asleep.

---

seven

---

Chanté woke up the next morning feeling exhausted.

She'd spent the entire night tossing and turning, but not because she was stressed like during midterms; it was the exact opposite, actually. All night, her dreams had been filled with thoughts of Asif — his hands, his mouth, the beautiful midnight of his jet-black hair, the feeling of his body pressed lightly up against hers, and then not so lightly. She'd replaced the stress dreams of exams with lust-filled fantasies, and while the latter was much preferred to the former, she was still sleep-deprived.

She woke up early the next morning with boiling blood in her veins and her pussy so wet her thighs were slippery with her own arousal. Thankfully, Chanté was a big fan of masturbation first thing in the morning.

And late at night.

And in the evening just before dinner.

And just after dinner.

Okay, Chanté believed in masturbation at all times and in all the ways, whether or not she had good material for her fantasies. Her cute crush on Asif was practically inspirational, especially now that she knew what the rough pads of his fingers felt like, grazing her nipple and brushing the baby hairs from her temple. She even knew what his strong grip felt like around her wrist, his warm breath tickling the curly hair at the nape of her neck, and his strong body almost pressed against hers, teasingly just out of her reach. These new details were like reading a new chapter of a textbook, adding shape and dimension to a thing she thought she'd understood. Apparently, shape and dimension just made her horny enough that the first thing she did after opening her eyes was roll over in bed, rummage around in her bedside table until she laid her fingers around a toy — any toy — and then shimmy out of her panties.

She closed her eyes and used the faint hum of her bullet vibrator to take her mind back to the bus stop last night.

Her unexpected date with Asif had been an emotional overload after weeks of dreaming about him, but for the purposes of her fantasy, she kicked it up a notch to get herself off as quickly as possible. She circled the blunt head of the vibrator over her clit slowly, softly, deliberately, while imagining Asif's hand slipping under her t-shirt like his fingers had invaded her bra last night. She felt his hand over her soft belly, his fingers playing at the crease of skin under her breast. Her own hand charted the same path. She toyed with her nipple almost absentmindedly and thumbed the toy to the next highest setting, jumping at the sensation.

She moaned and moved her toy down her slippery lips.

"Fuck," she breathed, bending her legs and spreading her thighs wider.

She pinched her nipple and then turned back to her bedside table, this time looking for another toy. She grabbed the small bottle of lube and the slim dildo she liked to use when her fingers weren't enough, and she needed to get off quick, fast, and dirty.

The small but powerful bullet hit her clit again, and she turned on the dildo as she pushed it inside her pussy, shivering violently in relief at the twin vibrations.

Chanté settled onto her back and returned to her fantasy.

There was a scene change. Now they were back at The Petal, in one of the private rooms at the back of the club. Chanté had served customers back there a few times, so she knew enough about the setup to create a serviceable setting for her masturbatory needs.

Asif was naked, which was against Petal policy, but it was her fantasy, so that was okay.

More than okay, actually.

She began to fuck herself with the slim vibrator while circling her clit with the bullet. She imagined herself dancing for Asif fully clothed. Well, what counted for fully clothed for one of the dancers early on in their set. She was wearing a black lace bodysuit, a piece she actually owned and had bought after a particularly great night of tips, when her head and her chest had been full up of the possibility that one day, she could be on stage. That was six months ago, and she hadn't even gotten up the nerve to wear that piece of lingerie yet. But the thought of wearing it for Asif made her entire body shudder and her back arch from the bed.

She thumbed both vibrators to their next settings.

His thighs were covered in the same dark hair as his head, and his hands were flat against his skin, and all that newly exposed hairy flesh was beautiful in Chanté's mind. She imagined herself sliding down the pole with her thighs wide and open to face him before turning and showing herself off for him. She bent forward, shaking her ass left to right in a gentle sway, just enough to get him excited, and maybe for him to see how excited thinking about feeling all that hair on his body had made her.

Chanté was close. She could feel the mother of all orgasms cresting. She bit her lips shut, and her groans were deep and desperate. But the fantasy was incomplete, and the orgasm she needed refused to come.

In her mind, that VIP room was silent. Asif didn't speak to her, and she didn't speak to him. There wasn't even any music. Slowly, her imaginary Asif frowned, and his formerly beautifully erect penis began to soften and wilt right in front of her eyes.

His face distorted into a mask of disappointment. She felt so ashamed, and suddenly, Chanté's desire withered away to nothing as well. She turned her toys off and pulled the slim vibrator from her body. She threw them onto the bed and stared at the ceiling.

She was out of breath and unsatisfied. What a terrible way to start the day.

"Chanté," Kenny called from the other side of her bedroom door, startling her.

"What? I'm awake. Leave me alone."

"So, you're in a good mood. Great. I'm heading out. I'm going to be gone all weekend, remember?"

Chanté sat up in bed and frowned at her closed bedroom door. "No, I do *not* remember," she said angrily, as if her forgetting Kenny's plans was his fault.

"Figured. I'm taking the new ROTC recruits to that team-building retreat. I'll be back Sunday afternoon."

"But," Chanté whined, "what am I supposed to do here all by myself?"

"Aren't you working this weekend?"

"Of course, I am. But not until tonight."

"Well," Kenny drawled. Chanté rolled her eyes, already knowing she was going to hate whatever common-sense thing he said next. "You are in college, so you could study. You could also use this pole you put directly in the middle of our living room with the promise that you would use it to get your routine together to audition for a dancer position at The Petal, but you haven't, and I know you haven't, even though you think I don't."

There was a heated silence as Kenny's run-on baring of her life hung between them.

"Don't you have to go?" she ground out.

"Oh, so you *do* remember," he laughed, and then knocked on her door twice in farewell. "Have a good weekend, roomie."

"Shut up," she said. "Be safe."

"You do the same. And use that damn pole carefully."

Chanté sat up in bed and listened as his booted feet carried him down the hall and out of their apartment before falling back onto her bed with a sigh.

"Use that damn pole," she whispered to herself.

ASIF'S first conscious thought was about Chanté.

This wasn't the first time, and he had no plans on letting it be the last. For a solid month, he'd blinked awake each morning with thoughts of Chanté filling his head, big and little. For someone who was generally not a morning person, this morning routine worked very well for him.

Asif groaned as soon as his palm made brief contact with his dick. He squeezed himself once as if to check his temperature and found himself very aroused, unsurprisingly. He reached for the lube he kept on the table beside his bed.

He poured the cool liquid onto the head of his dick and began to stroke himself. He kept his eyes closed. He didn't want to run the risk of ruining the fantasy he was weaving in his head, especially after last night.

In his mind, Chanté was wearing a version of the outfit she'd been wearing the night they'd met. That wasn't the first time Asif had seen her, of course, but being noticed by Chanté was so much better than just watching her through surveillance photos or from the dark corner of the club.

He tried to conjure just some of his favorite things about her; all her curves, the way he could tell her moods by the set of her lush mouth, how she used her big, brown eyes to push his emotional buttons, her attitude. He groaned, thinking about the way she could move from playful banter to firm negotiation to vulnerability and back again. More than once, he'd wondered if she was playing him and been charmed by the idea of it.

His back arched away from the bed as he tightened his grip on his shaft, imagining his hand was being directed by Chanté's command.

The Agency didn't have an express prohibition against masturbating about a waitress who worked at the establishment you were surveilling — but even Asif could understand that this was probably one of those unwritten rules they just assumed newbies like him would know. Oh, he knew; he just didn't care. Besides, no one would ever know what he'd been getting up to each morning, and if they did, he'd already decided that Chanté was worth the reprimand in his file.

She was more than worth it, actually, and the more he thought about that, the sloppier his strokes became. He wondered if watching him come undone just thinking about her would make Chanté happy. He wondered if she would bat his hand out of the way and show him how it was done with precisely executed strokes, designed to push him over the edge in no time. He didn't have to imagine that Chanté would never be as careless with his dick as he was. She struck him as the kind of person who gave serious consideration to everything, moving the chess pieces around the board of her life expertly, building the future she wanted piece by piece. She wouldn't take anything for granted. Not like him.

His phone dinged on the bedside table, and he grunted.

"Fuck." He was close and did not like being interrupted.

He kicked the covers from his body. His apartment was chilly, and the cold air shocked his muscles taut and made every pleasure receptor in his brain snap into focus. He sat up in his bed and pressed his bare back against the headboard, focusing now — the way he imagined Chanté would — on getting himself off. No more playing around. He was moaning with every stroke; the sensation of his own hand had taken on a new significance. He didn't just want to come; he wanted to come for Chanté.

"Fuck," he gasped around a puff of laughter at the thought.

His phone dinged again. He ignored it again. And again, and again.

He shut his eyes tighter and tried to re-focus on the images in his head.

Chanté hopping off the bus in front of the club in

her dirty sneakers and a coat that wasn't thick enough for Asif's liking. The serious scowl on her face. Her adorable mouth puckered in concentration. And then, the way that scowl would break into the brightest smile he'd ever seen. Chanté in high platform heels and jean shorts, her thighs jiggling with every step.

Asif had imagined himself on his knees between those thighs so many times he'd lost count.

He imagined their eyes meeting across the club, her beautiful glossy lips parting into one of those smiles while her eyes widened in surprise. All for him. The image wasn't sexual at all, not really, and yet that smile was what sent him over the edge.

It was just Chanté who made his back bow and his breath catch as his come spilled over his fingers to land messily on his stomach.

"Fuck," he groaned breathlessly, finally opening his eyes.

He sat, panting on his bed in this too-quiet room that wasn't his and didn't feel like home, his sweat and come drying on his overheated skin. His phone dinged again.

He groaned and reached for it with his clean hand. He was already preparing to tell Smith off for contacting him too early in the morning, but it wasn't Smith's number on his phone. It was Chanté's.

Asif sat up straight.

I don't have class today<br>
What are you doing?

He knew she didn't have class. Asif knew Chanté's entire school and work schedule because it was his job, of course. Not because he was stalking her, although he doubted she'd see it that way. But if he did his job well, she'd never have to know exactly how much he knew about her life or how much he'd had to lie to get as close to her as he already had.

He stared at her messages and felt dirty, covered as he was in sweat and come because of her, looking at a message from a phone number he already knew by heart even though she'd never given it to him.

His body shivered from the cold shame.

If Smith were here… Well, first, if Smith had been here, Asif would have been wearing clothes, and second, Smith would have reminded Asif that Chanté wasn't their target. She was just an incidental mark. They needed her for a small part of the plan, that's it. Smith would parrot Asif's briefings back to him like a good little soldier.

But Smith wasn't here, and Asif's problem — as had been noted in his personnel file — was that he had a bit of a problem with authority and following the rules. So, instead of ignoring Chanté's text message or calling it in, he balanced his phone in his left hand and carefully used his thumb to text her back, enjoying not having to lie to her whenever he could.

Thinking about you, of course.

He pressed send and jumped out of bed. He walked naked to the bathroom and used his dirty hand to turn on the shower, rinsing it under the spray as he waited for the water to warm. He was also impatiently waiting for Chanté to text back.

As usual, she was always unexpected.

Prove it.

Asif was not the kind of person who could be easily goaded into doing things he didn't want to do. It was one of the personality traits The Agency rated highly. So, when he aimed his cellphone camera at the wide mirror behind the bathroom sink, he knew exactly what he was doing, and he knew that it was in violation of more than a few rules. He just didn't care.

To be fair, the picture he sent Chanté was much tamer than it could have been. He was still naked, but the bathroom counter cut his body off just above his spent dick in the image. But that wasn't the point of this picture. He wanted her to see his come-covered stomach and know that he was filthy right now because of her.

He pressed send and jumped in the shower. As soon as he'd lathered his body and jumped under the spray, he heard his phone ding with another text message. If his skin flushed and his heart raced, wondering what Chanté's response would be to the image he'd sent her, at least he could lie to himself and blame it on the hot water.

Still, he rushed through the rest of his shower, washing his body and hair as quickly as possible. He didn't want to keep Chanté waiting.

When he was finished, he didn't even pretend as if he wasn't excited to check his messages. He was still dripping wet when he picked up his phone again. Her message was a simple command, and it made his dick hard. Actually, it made his entire body stiffen with desire. Chanté had texted him her address — not that he needed it — and two words.

Come. Now.

He knew what she meant, but the thought of her saying those words to him, maybe whispering them to him while wrapped around a pole, made him double over in excitement.

It was a bad idea to let himself feel this way about Chanté. He would have to lie to Smith. And he'd have to write pure fiction in every report he'd eventually file about this part of the mission. He'd have to say that he had been in complete control of his interactions with Chanté, even though he wasn't, not by a long shot.

On my way

He typed quickly.
Her response made him obnoxiously happy.

Good boy.

_______________________

eight

_______________________



This plan made sense to Chanté. She'd rolled it around and around in her head from every vantage point she could imagine before texting Asif.

Kenny had abandoned her to go play survivalist in the woods with his little camouflaged friends and had the nerve to tease her about not using her pole. Asif had *also* teased her about not using her pole while looking like the exact kind of pole she'd literally been dreaming of climbing. They were both correct — annoying, but correct — that she hadn't yet used the pole she'd special-ordered and then forced Kenny to help her install. And since she had the apartment all to herself, why shouldn't she invite Asif over to break her — she meant the pole — in?

Especially because he was going to pay for the pleasure.

It was perfect, so long as Chanté didn't let all the episodes of *Dateline* or the stories the dancers sometimes shared about creepy customers invade her head. If she did that, she'd have to acknowledge that this plan was *very* risky. Chanté liked to imagine that she wasn't scared of anything, but common sense told her that she should be very wary of strange men with pretty smiles, too much money, and an inexplicable interest in getting her alone.

But she didn't want to be afraid of Asif, even if she didn't quite know why. There was something about it that hit at some buried soft spot she hadn't yet covered with layers of armor yet. Something about the way he made her feel when his smile slipped away, and he was nothing but earnest conviction. Something about the way he believed that she could do this thing that she desperately wanted to do even though it terrified her.

Chanté wasn't afraid of much, but the pole and that stage made her heart beat faster and her mind race. She couldn't bat her eyes at the pole and tell it to go easy on her. She couldn't convince the pole to give her a leg up and stop her hands from slipping. She couldn't wink at the stage and persuade it to tell her how to win the crowd over.

She'd been hesitating to use her new pole out of fear that it would expose her deepest fear that actually, she couldn't do anything she set her mind to. Maybe getting out of Detroit had been a fluke, and after college, she'd go right back. Maybe she didn't have Caleb's strength or imagination. Maybe Chanté wasn't special after all. She couldn't tell Kenny that, though. Or Saraiya. And definitely not Asif. She needed to keep the mystique of power tight around her until it was real.

She jumped at the sound of a knock at her door.

Chanté finished wiping her pole down and tossed the microfiber towel in her hands onto the kitchen counter. She walked on shaky legs — a problem in her platform heels — toward the door. She looked through the peephole to make sure that it was Asif on the other side. It was, and he looked fine as hell.

She pressed her lips together and exhaled through her nose. "Who is it?" she called out.

She watched as a smile spread over his face, and he looked right at the peephole. "Who do you want it to be?"

Chanté relaxed and smiled back. "Someone with money," she said.

"Then let me in."

She unlocked her door and slowly pulled it open just enough to come face to face with Asif.

He looked more casual than at the club, wearing a pair of dark jeans, black running sneakers, and a plain black t-shirt. His hair was pulled into a short ponytail at the nape of his neck. He looked relaxed, which made Chanté realize how often he hadn't looked relaxed at the club.

"You look cute," she said.

"I was going for sexy."

"Sorry, you only achieved cute."

"They're not mutually exclusive," he said, leaning against the doorjamb.

Chanté tilted her head back and looked up at him. He was sexy. She wouldn't tell him that yet.

"I know. I'm cute and sexy," she said.

"I would have to agree. Are you going to invite me inside?"

Chanté felt her stomach clench, but she hid it under her dirtiest smile and lifted up onto the balls of her feet, a precarious stance in these shoes. "Are you going to make it worth my while?" she asked, her mouth just a hair's breadth away from his.

Chanté was wearing a pair of brown Lycra shorts pulled up over her belly button with a matching sports bra. This outfit was less about the skin it bared than the fact that it was skintight, and all of her curves were on display. But Asif's hand moved to the small patch of skin at her midriff. His knuckles kneaded gently into the small roll of flesh.

"Let me in, sweetheart," he whispered, leaning forward, dragging his lips across hers as he did.

"That's gonna cost you," she moaned into his mouth.

"Good."

---

CHANTÉ PUSHED THE DOOR OPEN, but she didn't move, and that made Asif smile.

She was nervous and trying to hide it with the dirty challenge in her eyes, and he liked that more and more about her every time they met.

He slipped into her apartment, brushing her body with his as he moved. He pretended not to hear her small intake of breath when they touched. He walked into her apartment and turned around as she shut the door. He didn't hear her turn the lock.

Smart girl.

It was a risk, inviting a virtual stranger into her apartment; a risk he would not have been happy that she'd made under any other circumstances, so he appreciated that she was taking precautions and leaving a road to escape as unencumbered as possible. Just in case. Chanté was safe with him, but she didn't know that, and he liked that she moved accordingly.

"This place is…" Asif said, his voice trailing off.

"Close to campus and affordable," Chanté finished for him.

He turned back around with a smile on his face and then tilted his head toward the pole in her living room. "And I'm assuming they have a lax policy on deposits here?"

"I know a guy who'll patch the holes for me," she said defensively.

"I'm sure you do. Shall we get down to business?"

Chanté didn't hesitate. "Two hundred for the dance."

Asif reached into his back pocket for his wallet, pulled out two crisp one-hundred-dollar bills, and laid them on the kitchen counter next to him. He put his wallet back in his pocket, reached into another pocket, and pulled out a wad of singles.

Chanté's eyebrows lifted.

"We should strive to make this as real as possible, I think," he said.

"Have a seat."

_______________________

nine

_______________________



Chanté had a playlist for this.

She'd spent more time working on the music she'd like to dance to than actually practicing, and now, she was standing in front of Asif with Rihanna's "You Da One" playing. She couldn't use this song if she actually got hired — Kay had a firm lock on all Rihanna songs at The Petal — but it was a good, slow song to build an easy bit of choreography to, even without practice.

Or at least, it should have been, but Chanté was frozen. She was standing with the pole between her and Asif, her heart was pounding a remix to the song against her rib cage, her stomach was doing cartwheels, and she could barely remember her name, let alone dance.

"Look at me," Asif said in a sharp tone.

Chanté lifted her eyes from the floor and scowled at him when they made eye contact.

"Atta girl," he said. "What's going through your head?"

She swallowed. "I-I'm…" She couldn't finish the sentence, and he didn't make her.

"Is it me?"

She shook her head.

"Is it the pole?"

She shook her head again but abruptly stopped.

"Ah. Come here."

"I'm in control here," she said, tightening her hands reflexively around the pole.

"I know. Humor me. Please."

It took her a few seconds to let go of the pole and step around it to walk toward him.

"Slower," he breathed.

Chanté paused for a second and took a deep breath. Asif took that deep breath with her.

"When you're ready," he said, watching her face. "If you can give me a private dance, you can do anything."

She took another deep breath and began to close the space between them, slowly steadying herself on her platforms with each step, elongating her short legs as much as possible. She kept her eyes on Asif's as she got closer.

"I should be working on the pole for my audition."

"We can work up to that. There's no rush."

"The auditions are next week."

He leaned forward and wrapped his hands around her legs, his fingers brushing the backs of her knees. Chanté jumped back with a laugh. "I'm ticklish."

"Good to know. Don't get all in your head. Don't worry about tomorrow or next week. Just be here in this moment with me." He reached out and brushed the back of his right hand up her shin.

"You wouldn't be allowed to touch me in the club," she said.

He wrapped his hand around her calf and squeezed. "Noted." He let her go in a lingering touch and sat back on the couch, scooting down and spreading his legs. "Stay with me," he reminded her.

Chanté nodded. She took another breath and checked in with herself. Her body felt loose and tight at the same time. She needed to relax, so she started moving from side to side in an easy sway to loosen her hips.

When she felt comfortable, she moved between Asif's legs and turned around, slowly lowering herself onto his lap.

He grunted.

She smiled and began to move her hips, circling her ass over the bulge in his pants.

He grunted again. "That's good."

"Shhh," Chanté said. "I'm getting in the mood."

"Sorry," he whispered.

Chanté placed her hands on Asif's knees and began to grind into him more purposefully, not quite on beat, but in a good, deliberate rhythm with varied pressure that made Asif's grunts turn to gasps and then back again.

It turned her on.

She knew it wouldn't be like this with all of her customers — probably not most of them — but she didn't have to think about that right now. Asif had given her permission to focus on what she felt while with him, and what she felt was a kind of desperate need for him that she'd never felt before, and she let it blossom.

Her fingers dug into his legs. She arched her back and threw her head back, moaning as her sex clenched, and she ground down on the much bigger mound in his pants.

"Fuck," Asif groaned.

"Shhh."

"Are you not in the mood yet?"

She straightened and turned to look at him over her shoulder, still moving over his lap. "It depends. Are you going to keep those singles to yourself?"

Asif blinked at her in a brief moment of confusion before lifting his hips. They both groaned. He rummaged in his pocket and pulled out the wad of bills.

"I was going to give it all to you anyway," he said.

"Make it real," she whispered and turned around again to grind on him.

"Fuck," he breathed, and then his fingers were at the waist of her shorts.

She felt the stiff bill he wedged there, and then his fingers brushed her waist before his hand went back to the couch.

Chanté stood and turned, swaying between Asif's legs as the song started over again. She was happy she'd put it on repeat.

Chanté lifted her hands to her breasts and ran her palms over her nipples before moving down her torso, over her stomach, and then between her legs. Asif's eyes followed the movement.

She bent forward, hiding his view, and he laughed, shaking his head.

He peeled another two bills from the stack in his hand and held them out for her. "Are you wet?" he asked.

Her fingers brushed along her slit. Her shorts were thin and didn't hide the warmth between her legs.

"That's gonna cost you more than two dollars," she moaned, circling her clit.

Asif lifted his ass from the couch and fished his wallet out of his back pocket. He pulled another hundred-dollar bill out.

"Yes," she breathed.

He nodded and shoved his wallet back into his pocket. "Come here," he said.

"Tsk tsk tsk."

"Please," he moaned.

Chanté stood straight and trailed her hands from between her legs across her thighs around to her hips. She turned and offered him her ass.

Asif smiled and leaned forward, tucking the bills in his hands into her shorts. "Thank you."

"You're welcome."

She turned back and crawled onto his lap, spreading her knees on the couch as wide as she could so she could press her pussy down onto his dick.

Asif's head flew back on another groan.

"Good?" she asked.

"Great," he corrected.

Chanté moved her hands to his chest. She pressed her palms to his body, enjoying the feel of him solidly under her fingertips. She moved her hands up to his shoulders and held on tight.

"Asif," she whispered, circling her hips.

"Fuck. Yes."

"How much money did you bring with you?"

He huffed out a laugh. "I have another two hundred-dollar bills in my wallet."

"I want them."

"They're yours."

"No," she said.

He lifted his head on a frown. His face was covered with a thin sheen of sweat. Chanté was sweating as well. "I'm going to earn them."

"Am I going to die in the process?" he asked. "No, don't answer that. Do what you have to do."

Chanté smiled and lifted up, scooting as close as she could get before sitting back on Asif's dick with a hard bounce that made them groan again. She moved a hand behind his head, gripping his small ponytail lightly between her fingers. "It'll be worth it, I promise."

"I know."

He made her feel powerful. He watched her with awe in his eyes as she ground on him, riding his erection slowly at first and then faster. Her labored breaths turned to moans, and Asif was nothing but grunts and gasps and blown pupils.

"I want to touch you," he wheezed after a while.

"I bet. Are you close?"

"Yes. Fuck."

She tightened her thighs around his waist, riding him, bouncing on top of him with purpose. Chanté lowered her mouth, hovering above his with a desperate, feral smile. "Can you..." Chanté licked her lips.

"Can I what? What do you want? What do you need?"

"I want you to come when I say," she said shyly.

He gave her a slack-jawed smile. "Whenever you're ready," he groaned.

"Come. Now," she said.

And he did.

—

ASIF COULDN'T REMEMBER the last time he'd come in his pants, but his last time hadn't been nearly as enjoyable.

He cleaned himself up as best he could in Chanté's bathroom. Thankfully, he'd worn all black, or else the wet spot on his pants would have been much more obvious. Walking in wet pants probably gave him away, anyway, but he did the best he could.

He took a few more minutes to snoop around the bathroom, not because there was anything useful to his mission in here, but just because he wanted to know her. So he opened the cap on what he thought was her body lotion and used some of it to moisturize his hands. And then he smelled her body wash since he was already being creepy.

When he came back into the living room, Chanté was in a pair of baggy black sweatpants and a t-shirt. All the money she'd earned had disappeared. She was in the kitchen, looking in her refrigerator.

"Were you being weird in my bathroom?" she asked.

"Of course, but only medium weird," he said.

She handed him a bottle of water with a smile and a shrug. "That's acceptable."

Asif took the bottle of water, twisted the top, and took a sip. She did the same with the bottle in her hand. They watched each other as they drank.

Asif put the cap back onto the bottle and then folded his arms and leaned forward on the kitchen counter. "Do you work tonight?" he asked.

She nodded. "You gonna come visit me?"

"Depends," he said, even though there was no doubt in his mind.

"On?"

"What time do you get off? Of work," he clarified.

She smirked. "Why?"

"Since we've committed to getting you ready to audition, I thought we could do a little research."

"What did you have in mind?"

"Who's that dancer you like?" he asked.

She was adorable when she blushed. "Her name's Joi," she said.

"I thought we could watch her together," he said.

"In one of the VIP rooms?"

"Would that make you feel more comfortable?"

She nodded. "But I can't do it while I'm on shift. I'm working the early shift, so I'll be off at nine. Can you...come then?"

Asif smirked at her. "I think I proved that I can

come whenever you want," he said, snatching the bottle of water and turning toward the door. "Thanks for the water."

He opened the door and turned to wink at Chanté over his shoulder. She rolled her eyes and giggled. That was Asif's favorite sound of the day.

He didn't call Smith until he was back in his car on the way to his apartment to change. "We're heading to The Petal tonight. Be ready for a brief at seven."

"Yes, sir. Anything I can do to prep before?"

"Yep. I'm going to need double the discretionary expense funds for tonight."

"Double?"

"Yep. Get started on the paperwork for me, will you? Thanks," Asif said and hung up before Smith could respond.

ten

Normally, Chanté was out the door at the end of her shift as fast as Saraiya would allow, but not tonight. She'd spent her entire shift feeling tense and nervous but also excited.

By the time Asif had walked in, she felt like a jittery, horny mess.

He was wearing another suit, this one a dark blue with a shirt so white it looked neon under the strobe lights and made the brown of his skin look…delicious.

Instead of taking over a booth, he slid onto a stool at the bar and watched her. Chanté could feel his eyes following her as she moved around the room. It was near the end of her shift, and she was wrapping up her customers and shifting her tables to Brittany, the new waitress whose name she'd finally learned.

She had one table left to close out. On the way, she turned to the bar and found Asif talking with Joi. Chanté's eyes widened; her mouth fell open in shock. Asif turned to see her watching him. He smiled and nodded in her direction. Joi turned, and they made eye contact.

Asif leaned and whispered in Joi's ear. Joi nodded.

Chanté turned quickly away and moved to her last table.

She scooped up the empty glasses. "Brittany'll take care of you for the rest of the night. Alright, ladies?"

"Thanks, Chanté," Sylvia said.

"Go home and rest. You can study in the morning," Evelyn said, and the rest of the table nodded along with her.

Chanté smiled at them. The Stud Players Bowling Team were some of her favorite regulars. "Will do. Y'all have fun."

"Oh, we will," Sylvia said with a wink.

Chanté waved and turned away, only to come face to face with Joi. "Hey," Chanté squeaked in shock.

"Hey. I'm Joi," she said.

"I know who you are," Chanté breathed. "I-I really like your sets."

Joi visibly relaxed. "Oh. Um. Thanks. Um, so your boyfriend said you were thinking of auditioning to be a dancer."

"My…boyfriend?"

Joi turned and pointed at Asif. He lifted his glass of cranberry juice in a toast and smiled.

"Ah. Yeah. My boyfriend," Chanté said.

"Is it true? The dancing, I mean."

"Um, yeah. I think. Maybe."

Joi's face relaxed into a sympathetic smile, and she nodded. "I get it. I was nervous too. He asked if I was interested in giving you two a private show. I'm down if you are."

Chanté took a deep breath. Her eyes flitted across the room to Asif. He was watching her like a hawk. She nodded. "I don't want it to be weird or anything."

"Girl, please. It won't. Besides, it'd be nice to have someone here who doesn't hate me just because Kay said so."

Chanté shook her head quickly. "I definitely don't hate you."

Joi grinned and nodded. "When are you off shift?"

"N-now. I just have to, um, clock out."

"Okay, then. I'll take your man back to the red room. Meet you there in five?"

Chanté nodded and turned to look at Asif. He winked at her and took another sip of his drink.

She walked back to the waitresses' locker room and clocked out. She opened her locker and hesitated. Should she keep her heels on? No, she decided definitively. Her feet were already sore, and even though this was research, it wasn't really work. She unstrapped her heels and shoved them into her backpack. And then she nearly fell while trying to tie up her tennis shoes.

She was nervous.

"Hey, girl, what's this I heard about you and your sugar daddy mackin' on Joi?" Angie said as she rushed into the room.

"What sugar daddy?"

"Fine, brown, money?"

"He's not my sugar daddy," Chanté sighed.

"Girl, why the fuck not? He's fine. Is brown. Has money. What more do you need?" Angie asked, opening her locker and pulling out her pack of cigarettes and lighter.

"I don't need a sugar daddy."

"You don't need money? 'Cause that's basically what you just said, and that don't make no sense."

"He's not my sugar daddy, and we're not trying to pick Joi up. I'm going to audition to be a dancer, and she's going to give me some pointers." Chanté's jaw was so tight she had to bite out each word.

"Mmmhmm, and he's there because…?"

"He's my boyfriend?" Chanté offered.

Angie stared at her as a look of disdain warped her face. "My story was better," she said with a shrug and walked out of the room for her smoke break.

Chanté shook her head and grabbed her lock from the locker. She wrapped it around the arm of her backpack and then pulled her bag on. Instead of following Angie to the exit, she walked down the small hallway back the way she came. At the end of the hallway, she could turn left and arrive back out onto the main floor or turn right to find another smaller hallway that led to three VIP rooms.

Well, two VIP rooms, and then at the far end was the new owner's office.

Chanté turned right and came face to face with Asif.

He was leaning his back against the wall outside the red room, halfway toward Mia's new office, with his hands in his pockets.

"My boyfriend," Chanté hissed.

Asif turned toward her with a mischievous smile on his face. "Close enough," he said.

She rushed to him and pushed him lightly. "Not close at all."

He turned his entire body toward her, still leaning against the wall. He bent forward and closed some of the space between them. She tilted her head back, thinking that it wouldn't be a bad thing if he kissed her right now.

"We needed a cover," he said.

"No, we didn't."

"Let's agree to disagree."

"I hate when people say that."

"Noted. Do your feet hurt?" he asked, looking down at her shoes.

She blinked up at him and nodded.

"I'll drive you home after this. Since I'm your boyfriend."

Chanté rolled her eyes and smiled. "My friend thinks you're my sugar daddy."

"Did you tell her you don't like that term?"

She shook her head. He leaned forward and brushed his mouth across her cheek, kissing her softly. "You look sexy tonight."

"I know. You look…sexy too."

He took a step back and smiled. "Oh, yeah? Not just cute?"

Chanté rolled her eyes and turned away as the door to the red room pushed open. Joi stepped into the hallway and smiled. "You two ready?"

Chanté opened her mouth, but all that came out was a high-pitched squeak when Asif's arms wrapped around her waist. He pulled her back into his body and kissed her cheek again. "Very. Aren't we, babe?"

Chanté scowled at him. "Babe? No way."

"Seriously?"

"Hate it."

Asif sighed. "Honey?"

"Ew."

"Come on. Sweetheart?"

"Absolutely not. We'll discuss this later," Chanté said and turned to Joi.

The woman had covered her mouth to muffle her laughter. "You two are cute," she said. "Come on."

Chanté scowled at Asif one more time before following Joi into the red room.

"Who doesn't like honey?" he mumbled, pulling the door shut behind them.

Chanté had been in the red room to drop off drinks, but it was different walking in here as a customer of sorts. Joi motioned for them to move to the leather couch. Chanté dropped her backpack on the floor and sat. Asif sat right next to her, wrapping his arm around her waist.

"Do you know how you two want to do this?" Joi asked.

Chanté turned to Asif with big, nervous eyes.

He squeezed her waist. "I was thinking that maybe you could dance for us, and Chanté can ask questions." He turned to her. "How does that sound?"

She nodded and turned to Joi. "I mean, if that's okay, with you?"

"Yeah. People say some wild shit to me while I dance. This is perfectly fine. Do you just want me to dance, or is this a *dance?*"

Chanté squinted her eyes in confusion. Once again, Asif was much faster to respond. "This is a dance," he said, pulling cash from his pocket."

"Completely naked?" she asked.

He counted a few hundred dollars and handed them over to her. "If you don't mind," he said nonchalantly.

Joi folded the money and slipped it into a small envelope on a table that also held the CD player for the room. She pressed play and moved to the pole in the middle of the room.

The distance gave Chanté a bit of space to breathe. Well, that, and Asif's fingers slowly massaging her hip helped her relax. She turned to him and whispered under her breath, "Touching's gonna cost you."

He smiled. "Worth it."

The room filled with Florence and the Machine's "Only If For a Night." Chanté's face lit up, and she turned to see Joi walking dreamily around the pole, with one hand circling it, casual but somehow sexy.

"You have the best music," Chanté called.

Joi smiled at Chanté and then grabbed the pole with both hands and lifted her body into the air. Chanté watched Joi move up the pole like an acrobat, graceful, careful, and slightly serpentine. The best thing about the dancers was all the ways they were different from one another, although she knew dancers like Kay didn't always respect dancers with different styles, like Joi.

"Um," Chanté said, far too low to be heard.

Asif's mouth was at her ear. "Louder," he commanded.

Chanté swallowed and nodded. Her voice was louder and shakier when she spoke. "What kind of upper body exercises do you do?" Chanté asked.

Ironically, Joi had wrapped her legs around the pole, and she looked as if she was sitting on air. Her arms were at her back. "I lift some weights. Nothing special," she said, and then her bra top loosened. She tossed it away.

Asif's fingers snaked under the hem of her shirt. Chanté shivered at his touch.

"Do you choreograph your own routines from beginning to end, or do you just feel it?"

Joi slid down the pole into a split on the floor. Asif and Chanté held their breath as she stretched the move out and leaned back on the floor before flexing her abs and returning to the pole.

"A little bit of both," Joi said. "Sometimes, I have an idea for the primetime shows. A whole concept, you know?"

Chanté nodded eagerly.

Joi leaned back, lifted her left leg, and moved it behind the pole to join her right. She turned from Chanté and Asif and lifted up to her hands and knees before moving up to just her knees. She looked at them over her right shoulder while bouncing her ass cheeks together and then separately. "But sometimes, I just be feeling a song, and I get on stage with no plan. It might help when you're new to have a little choreography just to get started."

"Okay," Chanté said. "I can do that."

"She sure can," Asif offered in a deep voice. Chanté licked her lips, remembering how good he'd looked on her couch while she'd writhed on top of him and he came in his pants, and then she forced herself to focus.

Joi unintentionally mirrored Chanté's grinding from this morning. She pulled the strings holding her bikini bottoms together with a smile. "Y'all are real cute. I wish I could find a man this chill."

Chanté turned to Asif, lifting her mouth uncon-sciously again, but this time, he heard the silent plea her body was making. He turned and moved his hand to her chin, angling her head at just the right angle, so when his mouth slanted over hers, she felt his kiss down to her toes. His mouth was warm, slightly tart, and sweet from the cranberry juice. His tongue was as playfully possessive as he was, teasing her own tongue into a dance and then letting her take control.

Chanté whimpered into his mouth, and he swiped his tongue along her lips, tasting her arousal. Joi's hands on Chanté's knees startled a moan from her, and Asif smiled as he licked that sound away as well.

His fingers moved to Chanté's chin, and he turned her head. They watched Joi in between Chanté's legs, her hands moving up Chanté's shins, over her knees, and between her thighs. Chanté was wearing a pair of fishnet stockings, and the pads of Joi's fingers brushed her skin here and there, heightening the intimacy of this moment.

Chanté balled her hands into fists and shoved them into the couch as Asif held her still, tightening his arm around her waist.

"Do you have other questions?" Joi asked.

"Do you regret coming to The Petal?" Chanté squeaked.

Joi stood, and Chanté's mouth watered at the sight of her up close and fully naked. She'd seen Joi naked plenty of times, but always in passing. As much as Chanté liked to watch the girls dance from the shadows of the bar, she usually only caught small snatches of their routines, and usually when they were dressed. It was surprisingly easy to clean up a table for turn-around or take a break to run to the bathroom when a woman was butt naked at the top of a pole, so she usually missed more than she liked.

And she'd missed a lot when it came to Joi.

Joi had a tattoo of a black panther that started at her right thigh with its front claws and roaring face. Its body moved up her side, and its tail wrapped around her back, curling around her left hip and thigh. It was beautiful and intricate, and up close, Chanté had the strongest urge to trace it with her tongue. And since Asif's tongue snaked out to lick at Chanté's right earlobe, she had the distinct feeling that he'd had a similar thought as well.

Joi moved her hand to Chanté's left shoulder and pushed her back onto the couch.

Asif let go of her, scooting back with her as Joi climbed onto Chanté's lap. "The money's better at The Petal," Joi said. "Everybody knows that. It was a business decision. I knew I'd have to work my way up from the bottom here." As she spoke, she gyrated on top of Chanté in small circles, and Chanté had a sympathetic moment where she realized all that she'd put Asif through this morning.

She wondered if she should have charged him more.

Joi turned to Asif and smoothed a hand over his chest. "This is Kay's house. Or at least, it was until Saraiya sold it. Maybe the new owner will be good for me."

"Why do you think that?" Asif asked.

"You sure you want to hear this?"

Asif's eyes darted to Chanté, and she nodded.

"So adorable," Joi mumbled and then leaned forward, smothering Chanté for a brief second with her breasts. She smelled like fresh strawberries. She moved back and then climbed off of Chanté's lap to crawl into Asif's.

Chanté's pussy clenched, and she rubbed her legs together, a move that Joi clocked. She ground her pussy onto Asif's lap with a satisfied grin. "So y'all get down like that, huh?"

"Yeah," Chanté breathed. She could see Asif smiling at her out of the corner of her eyes.

Joi turned to Asif. "I like Saraiya, but she shouldn't be fucking her employees. It's a bad look, especially when it goes bad. That's the only reason Kay acts like she does. If the new owner is about her business, Kay'll be out of here sooner than later, and someone's gotta take her place."

Chanté shifted closer, rubbing her hand over Asif's chest. "But did you see the way Saraiya was looking at the new owner during that meeting?"

Joi rolled her eyes and shook her head. "Girl, yes. They definitely fucking."

"I knew it."

"Why do you want to dance?" Joi asked Chanté, still grinding into Asif.

Chanté thought about lying or saying something dirty and flirty, but she didn't want Joi to think she was disrespectful, and she didn't want to lie to Asif.

"I think it's beautiful. When y'all are up there, you just look so..." Chanté's voice trailed off in a smile. "You look like the world should fall at your feet."

Asif's hand dug into Chanté's hair. He pulled her mouth to his, kissing her, moaning as Joi worked him over. And then Joi's hand was running down her back to her ass, squeezing her, touching her the way The Petal officially did not allow.

Asif pulled Chanté's head back, and Joi's mouth covered hers.

"Fuck," Asif breathed.

He was coming. He'd only come for her once, but the sound of his cursing grunt and his body shaking underneath her wasn't a thing Chanté would soon forget. Nor was the taste of Joi's tongue in her mouth, her strawberry lip gloss gliding over Chanté's lips, and Asif's hand in her hair, holding Chanté in place.

Joi kissed Chanté until Asif stopped shuddering beneath them. She swiped her thumb over Chanté's mouth to wipe away some of her gloss with a smile. "If you two have any more business questions, you know where to find me," she said and crawled from Asif's lap.

Chanté and Asif were panting on the couch as she collected her clothes and CD. She stopped at the door, still naked, with a smile on her face. "And if you're interested in anything not business-related," she said, "y'all know where to find me for that, too."

She pushed out of the VIP room, and they sat there for a few more seconds in silence.

"I really should have brought a change of pants," Asif said.

Chanté dissolved into a fit of giggles.

---

"DOWN HERE?" Asif asked, pointing at a door he already knew led to an employee bathroom.

"Yes, and make it quick," Chanté said. "Customers aren't allowed back here."

"A quickie?"

"Oh my god," Chanté said with a roll of her eyes. He pushed the bathroom door open as she stomped away.

Inside the bathroom, Asif checked the two stalls. Once, on his first mission, he'd thought a bathroom was empty and been very wrong. Although, convincing a woman that, of course, a plumber would show up at a fancy restaurant in a tuxedo to unclog a toilet had taught him the valuable lesson that someone vaguely interested in fucking you would believe almost anything, even the ridiculous.

He locked the bathroom door, plucked his earbud from his breast pocket, and put it in his ear.

He cleared his throat to announce that he was

online, but he didn't speak just in case someone was walking by, or Chanté had doubled back.

"You there?" Smith asked.

Asif sighed in frustration.

"Okay. Great. So how was the dance?" Smith asked.

Asif didn't answer because he couldn't. If he could have, he would have cursed Smith out at the top of his lungs, so he gave him the silent treatment and turned on the bathroom sink. He also carefully climbed onto the toilet nearest to the bathroom's far wall. Asif had been staring at the blueprints to this building for weeks before he'd ever even stepped foot in The Petal. As he'd stood outside of the red room waiting for Joi to set up and for Chanté to clock out, he'd tried to map this hallway onto the blueprints he knew practically by heart.

If he could have risked it, he would have ducked into Mia's office, but his eyes caught on the domed security cameras over the door and at the other end of the hallway. Maybe he could have gotten lucky, and whoever was supposed to be watching those cameras had left their post. He could have broken into the office and at the very least planted a bug somewhere inside. It might have taken a while, and maybe Chanté might have wondered where he had gone, but maybe he could have concocted some lie to explain his absence.

When Asif filed the brief about tonight, he would

leave a lot off the page, like the way his stomach leapt in his gut when he walked into the club and saw Chanté gliding across the floor. Or the way he'd felt an unfamiliar sliver of jealousy when she'd smiled at a customer who wasn't him. He wouldn't share that stroking Chanté's soft roll over the top of her shorts calmed him or that he'd been nervous while Joi had been dancing, afraid that maybe she would convince Chanté not to audition. No one at The Agency needed to know the need that dug its claws into his soul as soon as Chanté's lips finally crashed into his, and she moaned into his mouth. The heated moments they shared with Joi were his and Chanté's and Joi's alone.

But he also wouldn't share that the reason he hadn't broken into Mia Malkova's office when he had the chance was because he didn't want to have to look into Chanté's face and lie, and he didn't want anything he did to get back to her. No, he'd write something up about there not being time and the likelihood that someone assigned to monitor the security cameras in a strip club was *unlikely* to leave their post.

"Okay," Smith said, finally catching up. "All you have to do is put the device in the vent, and the tech team'll take over."

Asif grunted. It actually wasn't as easy as that. He kept a Swiss army knife on his key ring for any number of uses, like, for instance, unscrewing old rusty screws keeping an air vent grate attached to a wall with crumbling plaster. Asif tried not to think about the seconds ticking by as he slowly worked two of the screws loose. Time was always the enemy, and Asif was of the mindset that it was better ignored whenever possible.

Once he could slide the vent grate out of the way just enough, he reached into his jacket pocket for the device the tech team had given him. Asif thought it looked like a toy of some kind, but he wasn't in tech for a reason. Before he placed the cube in the vent, he pressed down on a button that was nearly imperceptible, and a green light started to blink; the rest was in the hands of whatever sixteen-year-old hackers on parole The Agency employed to do their dirty work.

He screwed the vent back into place and grunted once more.

"Signal received," Smith said. "See you back at base."

"Actually, I'll see you tomorrow," Asif said. "I'm driving the waitress home."

"Um…"

"Go home," he said and pulled the earbud from his ear. He screwed the grate back into place and hopped to the floor. At the sink, he unzipped his pants, grabbed some paper towels from a stack next to the sink, wet them, and made a half-assed attempt at cleaning himself. There was a knock on the door as he was washing his hands.

"Asif?" Chanté's voice was soft, wary, unsure, and

Asif knew he'd made the right decision not to break into Mia's office earlier.

He quickly dried his hands and opened the door. "Miss me?" he teased.

She smiled. "You wish," she said and then yawned.

"I do," he whispered. "Come on, let's get you home. Did you eat dinner?"

"Depends."

He sighed. "Yes, I'm buying. Obviously."

"Oh, great, I'm starving," she giggled, leading him toward the side exit.

---

eleven

---

The next week flew by, and Chanté wasn't happy about it.

Sure, she spent a good portion of those days in her living room in skintight clothing dancing for Asif, watching him watch her as she tentatively felt her way around the pole, testing different ways to hold it and wrap herself around it and crawl up and slide down, watching his face to see what he liked and didn't. Although, as far as she could tell, Asif liked everything she did. The trick was to listen to her and Kenny's old couch as it creaked under his shifting weight and to watch his hands. Asif always held his money in his left hand and placed his right on his thigh. Did he grip his thigh? Then he liked what he saw. Did his thumb caress the outline of his dick through his jeans? Then he was happy.

And if Asif littered the carpet at his feet with dollar bills? Then Chanté knew that he was very happy. And even though she wouldn't admit it to anyone, there was something about making Asif happy that made Chanté nearly giddy.

Her savings account was feeling pretty great as well.

Still, she wanted that week to last forever, but it didn't.

Asif answered the phone on the third ring. "Are you naked?"

"That's not a greeting," she sighed. Chanté was walking across campus to her engineering class. She was seriously considering sitting on a bench and just staying there, skipping class and work, and most crucially, the audition. And then she'd had the idea to call Asif.

"I beg to disagree. How's it going, beautiful?" he asked tentatively.

He'd tried out different terms of endearment after that night at the club, and *beautiful* seemed to be the only one that didn't make her roll her eyes, so he'd settled on it easily. Every time it fell from Asif's lips, Chanté's mouth lifted into a small smile, the only outward sign of the secret internal thrill it gave her.

"The audition's tonight," she said.

"I know. Do you need another practice session? Because if you do, I'm certain I can make time for you," he said, his voice dropping to a whisper that sounded like deep, rich molasses.

It was a tempting offer. "I can't. I have class in twenty minutes and some annoying meeting for a group project."

"Ugh, I hated group projects in college."

"Exactly. I won't be free until it's time to go to work, and then…"

"The audition. It's okay to be nervous, you know?"

"No, it's not," Chanté said. "And I'm not nervous."

"Oh, no, of course not. But if you were, that would be alright. And I wouldn't tell anyone." This time, when he whispered, it was sincere. She loved when he spoke to her like that — as if whatever was between them wasn't purely transactional. Sometimes, Chanté even felt as if it wasn't.

"If I was nervous," she said.

"Big if, but we can pretend."

Chanté's eyes stung with happy tears. She didn't know why she was on the verge of crying, or maybe she just wasn't willing to admit it. "If I was nervous, and I needed a pep talk, would you give me one?"

"Yes."

"What would it sound like? Not that I need it. Just so I know."

"Of course."

Chanté heard a door closing on Asif's end. "If you

needed a pep talk, I'd tell you that the world is completely at your feet."

"My bus pass and final exams beg to differ."

"It might not seem like it right now," Asif said, smoothly pushing through her self-deprecating interjection. "I know how easy it is to listen to only the bad things you've heard about yourself. And because you're such a smart ass, you always think you're right."

"I—"

"Chanté," Asif warned.

"Sorry."

"You might be right about a lot of things. Most things, even."

"Thank you," she whispered, and he laughed on the other side of their connection.

"But the things most of us struggle to see are usually right in front of us, especially about ourselves. If you don't trust yourself right now, trust me. It's just like that first dance. Focus on me because I see you clearly."

"You do?"

"I do. You're a smart ass who likes to flirt her way out of letting other people see you. You won't just be stripping your clothes off on that stage, and it's understandable to be terrified of what will happen if you peel back all that armor you've built. But as someone who's peeked past your defenses the smallest bit, you should know that I know you're fucking beautiful.

You're even more beautiful when you're completely naked… I mean emotionally, but if you have a second, I would also like to talk about how great I'm certain you are while naked physically in amazing detail."

Chanté burst into laughter. She'd made it to her classroom, but instead of going inside, she strolled to the end of the hall and perched on a windowsill while other students rushed past. "I've got three minutes before I'm late," she laughed.

Asif sighed. "Three minutes? Ugh, that's not enough time, but I guess I can start. I'll finish tonight."

"T-tonight? Are you…coming to the audition?"

"Oh, honey… I mean beautiful," he corrected quickly. "I wouldn't miss it for the world."

▭

briefing

"SORRY ABOUT THAT," Asif said, walking back into the conference room where his team was being briefed.

"Everything alright?" Parker asked. He was the regional head of this operation. Asif knew that he'd been assigned to follow Mia Malkova on his orders, and he guessed that decision had been made because no one *really* thought Mia was a good lead. Even now, as they were planning to make their move on The Petal and probably acquire all the information they needed to take a real shot at the Malkova family's operations because of his work, he could feel that there were people in this room who didn't think he was good enough to be here.

"Yep. Just a little asset management," he said, the words souring on his tongue.

"Alright. Well, we're almost done here, so let's wrap it up. The tech department has been able to do a lot of great work in the last week, much more work than many people in this room."

Asif saw a few agents with far more time on the job than him shift in their seats, but he refused. He stared at Parker, and when the two made eye contact, he made sure not to blink. And when the other man looked away first, Asif felt some small, petty triumph in his chest.

"The audio recordings they've been able to get from our probe in the vents have been surprisingly clear. Now we could take those recordings to Yuri Malkova and see what he does with definitive proof that his daughter is planning a takeover, but that's unlikely to get us anything besides yet another missing, probably dead woman. What we need is leverage." Parker turned to Asif with a barely polite smile. "And that's where you come in."

Asif nodded and turned toward the rest of the

table. "There are a lot of variables at play, but we know for sure that Mia Malkova will be at the auditions for the possible new dancers."

"Lucky her," someone muttered from across the table.

Asif clenched his fist and took a deep breath before continuing. "Most of the dancers will be on the floor to watch the new recruits. It's apparently quite competitive. With the backstage largely empty, we hope, I'll sneak into Mia's office."

"All we need you to do is plug this USB into her computer, and we'll do the rest," one of the tech agents said, holding a small device in the air.

Asif nodded.

"How are you going to get out?"

"I'm not," Asif said. "That's the beauty of the setup. They've seen me at The Petal before with Chanté. Once I've planted the USB, I'll go watch her audition like nothing is wrong."

"Lucky you," that same person muttered, and some of the agents behind Asif started snickering like schoolchildren.

Asif stood from the table. "Well, we can't all specialize in jacking off the egos of sweaty day traders with coke habits," he said and then walked from the room.

## twelve

Angie had been staring at Chanté for a solid five minutes with a look of confusion on her face. She'd thought her friend was annoyed that she was auditioning to be a dancer. She was wrong.

"I kinda thought you'd wear something much more…"

Chanté crossed her arms and scowled at Angie. "More what?"

"Less," Angie corrected. "You're practically covered head to toe. You do know what kind of establishment we are, right?"

Chanté rolled her eyes. "It sounds like you're calling me slutty."

"No, I'm asking why you don't look sluttier. I feel like you really missed the mark here."

"I know what I'm doing?"

"I mean, you know I love you, and I normally would believe you, but—"

"Will you let the experience unfold?"

Angie perked up with a smile on her face. "Oh? There's gonna be an experience?"

"Obviously," Chanté said. "Now leave me alone, okay?"

Angie grabbed her cigarettes and threw her hands up in surrender. "My bad, girl. You're already acting like them," she teased. "But I'm rooting for you. I'm fucking with you, but I'm rooting for you."

"Thank you," Chanté whispered.

Angie winked at her and then went outside for her smoke break.

The auditions were set to start in fifteen minutes. Because she already worked at The Petal, Saraiya had promised Chanté that she could go near the middle of the group, far enough down the list that she could get a sense of her competition, but not dead last, just in case her nerves got the best of her. But ever since Chanté had arrived at The Petal, her nerves had been winning the battle, and Chanté was seriously considering backing out of all this.

Her phone rang. Chanté pulled her locker door open, her stomach flipping at the thought that it was Asif calling to tell her that he was here.

It was Kenny.

"Hey," she said.

"Hey. Don't worry."

"I'm not worried."

"Okay," he said, disbelief dripping from the word. "Anyway, I'm sorry I can't make it. I tried to get my shift at the grocery store changed."

"Don't apologize. Just make it up to me with a cake from the bakery."

"Way ahead of you. I pulled that double chocolate fudge cake you like aside as soon as I clocked in."

"You're the best best friend, you know?"

"I do. And you're going to be great."

"Thanks, Ken Doll."

He sighed. "I really hate that nickname."

"Do you? Or are you still adjusting to being the hot dude on campus?"

"I'm hanging up now."

"Thanks for calling," she whispered.

"Bye, roomie."

Chanté hung up the phone, and the sound of Saraiya's voice rang out in the hallway. "Let's get it started, ladies! Everybody out front."

Chanté shuddered and checked her text messages again, hoping there was a chance she'd just missed a message from Asif.

"You ready?" Saraiya asked, poking her head into the locker room.

Chanté swallowed slowly and then nodded quickly. "I think I'm freaking out a little bit."

"A little bit isn't bad. But if you're gonna throw up, get it out now. I do *not* want to be cleaning puke off the stage again this week," Saraiya said loud enough for all the other dancers to hear, including the other auditioning dancers.

Chanté shoved her phone into her backpack, slammed her locker, and pressed her lock closed. She took another deep breath and straightened her back.

She took one step toward the door. When her Perspex heel hit the stone floor, it centered her, reverberating up her leg, making her thigh jiggle gently. The next step was even better.

Asif was right; Chanté's armor was strong. It had gotten her out of her parents' houses, through all the group and foster homes, and it was getting her through college, even though every day she worried that she wasn't supposed to be there. And it was going to get her through this damn audition. She wouldn't worry about what would come after, how her life could change if she got the job, or how she would feel if she didn't. That was for later.

In the hallway, she ran into Joi. She'd seen her once or twice around the club since that VIP room experience, and every time they came face to face, Chanté thought about Joi naked in Asif's lap, and it made her skin warm.

Joi was barely covered in a fringe mini dress that shimmered, flashing her naked figure underneath with every step. Chanté's mouth fell open. Joi's eyes traveled down Chanté's body with a smirk. "Break a leg, Chanté," Joi said as she passed. "Make your boyfriend and me proud."

A small squeak was the only reply Chanté could muster.

"HO-LY SHIT," Smith breathed into Asif's ear just as the side door closed behind him.

Smith was sitting at the bar in The Petal's main room. It was his job to let Asif know just as soon as Chanté and Mia Malkova entered the main room. Technically, Asif only needed to know about the latter, but he wanted to know about Chanté. He'd asked the other man to describe what she looked like.

Not what she was wearing, unfortunately, but her face. Was she frowning or smiling? How big was her smile? Was she bouncing on the balls of her feet? Why the fuck was he looking at her ass? Did she seem to be looking for anyone? For him?

He didn't ask those last two questions. They were too personal, and this was business. Who cared that he'd crossed so many lines with Chanté over the last week? Not the ones people probably assumed he'd crossed, but the ones that mattered to him, at least. And in the end, Asif's curiosity about Chanté had opened the door to Smith's shocked chattering under his breath as he experienced a strip club as if it was the first time.

The tech team had finally managed to hack into the security system. They'd cloned the camera feed and given Asif a conservative ten minutes before it was likely someone noticed that something was wrong. Asif thought he could probably stretch that to twenty minutes for the same reason he hadn't broken into Malkova's office last week. The likelihood that whoever was monitoring The Petal's security cameras was watching the empty backstage area when everyone in the club was out front was slim, but he wouldn't press it if he didn't have to.

Thankfully, there was no one backstage, so Asif could tell him to, "Shut up over the fucking line," for the first time with relish.

But that was all he said.

He moved through the backstage area cautiously but casually. He was dressed in another suit, just like he'd been every other time he'd visited The Petal, and he walked as if he was supposed to be back here.

Asif stopped at the forked hallway. To his left, he could hear the club. The deejay was getting the auditions started. He could hear the excited rustle of the crowd. He imagined that Chanté was sitting by herself, smiling absently at the stage as if none of it really mattered, on the outside. Meanwhile, she was probably an adorable ball of nerves on the inside.

He wished someone else could have done this bit so he could have sat next to Chanté and made her laugh. The thought made him feel guilty, and he propelled himself to the right, down the hallway that led to the VIP rooms and Mia's office.

He reached into his pocket for the lock-picking set, and when he found her office door locked as he'd expected, he went to work. He kept one ear on the lock and the other on the hall behind him. He heard the lock click, and he tried the handle.

"In," he breathed when it turned.

"Take your time," Smith breathed.

Asif rolled his eyes and slipped into Mia's office.

The office was plain, almost as if Mia had never really moved in. She probably hadn't, he thought to himself. If he were in her shoes, he would have leaned into the idea that this club was her playground, not serious business. But the desktop computer on her desk in the middle of the room gave away her intentions.

"Does the computer need to be on?" Asif muttered.

"I don't know," Smith answered.

"Then don't speak," Asif hissed.

"No," the tech agent from the briefing meeting earlier responded. "But if you can wake it up, that would save us a few seconds."

"Gotcha."

Asif moved to the desk and found the first empty USB port. He reached into his pocket, pulled the USB stick out, and inserted it. Once he'd pushed it in place, he realized that it was so small that it was nearly impossible to see.

"Damn, that's small," he said.

"Most people won't notice it if they're not expressly looking for it. Can you wake the computer, agent?"

"Oh, yeah. Sorry." Asif moved around the desk and pressed the space bar with two of his knuckles.

The computer monitor turned on, lighting up the dark room. Everything looked normal for a second, and then the tech team took over.

"Thank you, agent. We got what we need."

"Get out of there," Parker said in an officious tone.

"Coming."

"So is Smith, probably," someone said over the line, clearly by accident.

"Whoever said that should report to my office first thing in the morning," Parker said.

Asif smiled and made his exit. He peeked out into the hallway, locked the door, and then exited.

One thing they told you at every level of your training was to never get cocky, and that was always a struggle for Asif; he was cocky by default. But cockiness didn't kick Asif's ass this time; it was excitement.

He'd done what he needed to do; the rest of the

mission wasn't his concern. And now that he was free, all he wanted to do was get out there and see Chanté's audition. He was rushing toward the fire exit, so he could walk around to the front of the building like a regular customer.

"What the hell are you doing back here?" a voice called.

Asif hadn't met him, but he knew that was the club's security guard. Chanté said his name was Stevie. Asif could see the door ahead of him; it was close enough that if he sprinted, he could probably be halfway down the alley before the older man even made it outside. But if he did that, he couldn't turn right around and come back into the club. Even if he was willing, Parker wouldn't allow it, and he'd be right.

So, as much as Asif didn't want to turn around, he did. Anything not to jeopardize being some small part of Chanté's moment.

"I'm sorry," Asif said, turning around slowly and coming face to face with the security guard.

Stevie's hand was on the baton in his utility belt. His face was distorted in a frown. He squinted at Asif and then reached into his chest pocket for his glasses. Asif waited patiently, smiling serenely at the man. "Oh," Stevie exclaimed once his glasses were in place. "Aren't you Chanté's sugar daddy?"

"She prefers patron," he said.

"A what?"

"Boyfriend," Asif said.

"Alright. What are you doing back here?"

"She's auditioning today."

"Not back here."

He smiled and nodded. "I know, but I can't stay long after her audition, and I brought her this."

Asif reached into his back pocket and pulled the small thin gift box out for the man to see.

"And what's that now?"

Asif swallowed. "She doesn't wear jewelry," Asif said. It was one of the first things he'd noticed about her. She didn't have any rings or necklaces, nothing. He'd thought it was because she wasn't a jewelry person, but the more he'd gotten to know her, that didn't quite make sense. Finally, it hit him like a ton of bricks out of nowhere. No one had ever given Chanté a piece of jewelry, and if nothing else, Chanté seemed like the kind of person to whom that would matter.

So, Asif bought Chanté a solid gold anklet crusted in diamonds. Something dainty and expensive. Something that would remind her of him when he was gone.

"Just something to celebrate the occasion, no matter what happens."

Stevie nodded at him slowly. "Her locker's in here," he said, pushing a door open.

"Thanks," Asif said.

When he was in the small room, Stevie pointed at a locker. "That's hers."

"Hmm," Asif said.

"You can put it through the slat," Stevie offered helpfully.

"Thanks," Asif said and did as the older man suggested.

"You better get out front. She should be going up soon."

"Can you not tell her I was back here?"

Stevie shrugged. "She'll figure it out eventually, I guess. Get on out."

"Thank you," Asif said and jogged toward the fire exit. Outside, he exhaled loudly.

"Hey, boss, they just called your girl up," Smith said seriously.

"Fuck. Fuck. Fuck."

<hr>

"COMING TO THE STAGE, it's The Petal's own ball of fun, Chanté," DJ Demetrius said.

Chanté scowled across the club at him. He cringed as if he realized how annoying that introduction was as soon as the words left his mouth.

"My bad," he muttered into the microphone, but he didn't take it back.

"Jerk," Chanté mumbled. "Never giving his ass free drinks again."

She was standing off to the side of the stage, and

her nerves felt like a whole fucking herd of stampeding gazelles in her stomach. She thought that maybe she should have taken Saraiya up on her recommendation and at least tried to throw up. It was too late for that now, though.

She stepped gingerly onto the stage and walked to the pole at the far end, closest to the crowd. She'd been on the other side of this stage at least three nights every week for almost a year and a half, and she'd always assumed that the dancers couldn't really see what was happening on the floor because of the lights. She was wrong. The spotlights obscured her vision of the ceiling, but down below, at the tables, her vision was clear. It made sense. Who gave a shit about the ceiling when the money was at her feet? Or at least the money *would be* at her feet if she could stick this fucking audition. But she didn't think she could. Not with Saraiya and the new owner sitting in the front row, looking blandly up at her. They were all she could see. Chanté couldn't even pick Joi out of the crowd.

And where the fuck was Asif?

Chanté blinked back tears, which only made her angrier that he'd told her he would be here, but he wasn't.

And then, of course, he was. Of fucking course, he would make an entrance.

Chanté watched as Asif strode into the club and walked directly to the front of the stage. He picked up a chair on his way and planted it directly in front of her. He unbuttoned his jacket and sat casually in the chair, looking up at her like she was the only other person in the room.

Chanté blinked back happy tears and nodded at Demetrius, finally ready to begin. There was a lot at stake with this dance, but Chanté didn't let herself feel it. In her mind, there was only Asif, and this dance was for him.

CHANTÉ WAS STANDING CENTER STAGE, both hands clutched nervously around the pole. She was covered from her neck to her ankles in a skintight black bodysuit. He hadn't expected that. In her living room, that would have been great, but in the club, her outfit hid her assets.

Asif felt a moment of panic that this was a mistake.

Katy Perry's "Wide Awake" started playing.

The lights cut out.

Asif started laughing, and the crowd actually gasped.

"Of fucking course," he breathed, smiling up at Chanté's bodysuit. Under a low spotlight, he and everyone in the audience could see that it was suggestively see-through and covered in sparkles.

It wasn't the most revealing outfit, and some would

say it wasn't the sexiest. But Asif thought it was the most Chanté outfit he could have imagined.

He sat in his chair, riveted as she slithered up the pole and then lowered into a squat with spread legs. He shifted in arousal as she crawled on all fours toward him and then writhed suggestively on her back.

The dim lights lifted slowly as the song played on. By the second chorus, Chanté was on her knees with her back to the audience. Asif leaned forward as she crossed her arms around her front and began to pull her bodysuit apart. The sparkling black depths had reminded Asif of constellations, and her light brown skin was like crashing down to earth in a bed of soft grass.

As she uncovered her back and shoulders and just the suggestion of her breasts, he felt as she was baring herself for him. As if this entire dance was choreographed for him, and not because she was getting naked, and that was the one thing she hadn't done during all their practicing, but as if it was an olive branch. It was like she was offering herself to him if he wanted her.

It broke something in Asif to witness this figurative invitation and know that he couldn't take it.

No, that wasn't entirely right. He *could* accept everything she was offering here; not just her body, but a space in her life, sex, everything — but he wouldn't. He couldn't do that to her.

The song ended with Chanté balanced on her tail bone, one arm covering her breasts, and a soft, shocked look on her face.

The crowd rioted.

"Play the song again," someone yelled.

"That better not be it."

Chanté met Asif's eyes, and they were sparkling at him.

"She did that on purpose," Mia Malkova said behind Asif.

"I told you she was smart," Saraiya said.

"We'll see. She'll bring in money for sure."

"For sure."

Asif stood from his chair and winked at Chanté before turning and walking out of the club. The mission was over. He'd probably never see Chanté again. She'd hate him, and eventually, she'd realize that was a good thing.

thirteen
TWO MONTHS LATER

"I been hearing about you, girl," Miss Francine said as soon as Chanté stood behind her, hitching her backpack on, ready to sprint from the bus when it stopped outside of the club.

"Good things?"

"Yeah, girl. They said that artsy shit you're doing on stage is real sexy."

"I try," Chanté breathed.

"Ain't no try, girl. You doin', and you know Miss Francine is proud of you."

Chanté blushed. Francine had been saying some version of this nearly every time Chanté saw her on the way to work. Maybe some people would have thought it was overkill, but not someone who was as starved for positive attention as Chanté was. She tried not to lean into that gaping hole. She'd been to enough group therapy as a kid to know that she couldn't fill the hole her parents had left with other people.

Sometimes she slipped up, though.

"You alright?" Miss Francine asked.

"I'm fine. Just tired. The new semester is kicking my ass already."

"Oh, and these late nights can't help."

Chanté shrugged. "I'm already used to that. I just need to get back in the groove of things."

Chanté hated lying to Francine. She was one of her favorite people, but she didn't want to talk about Asif with anybody. Actually, she wanted to talk about Asif with everybody, but no one in her life knew him besides Joi, Angie, and Stevie, somehow.

She might have spoken to any of them in the past two months since Asif had disappeared, but life at The Petal had been *very* strange.

Chanté and two other girls had gotten invitations to dance at The Petal immediately after the auditions. Two days later, Saraiya had shown up to work drunk and raging. Kay had been the only one who could talk her down — which had pissed Pebbles all the way off and led to a fight on stage in the middle of Chanté's first actual shift as a dancer. One of the new girls had walked out immediately at that and started telling anyone who would listen that The Petal was ghetto as hell. Joi had had the bright idea to choreograph a wet wrestling set, and the customers had come streaming in to see that show and gauge how ghetto it was for themselves.

And then the Feds showed up one night and ransacked the new owner's office. That was the first time Chanté realized that the new owner had basically fallen off the face of the earth since the audition. *Very weird*. Angie and the other waitresses were working on a theory that Mia had been in the mob. They'd joined with a few regular customers to launch a group investigation that didn't really amount to much besides chatting on slow nights and watching a few minutes of the evening news.

Saraiya eventually came back to The Petal, and the investigation turned to intense scrutiny of the Saraiya/Kay/Pebbles love triangle.

In the meantime, Joi had quietly taken over as The Petal's hottest attraction. It wasn't the way she'd planned, but Chanté was in awe of her ability to take an opening and run with it all the way to the bank.

Chanté wanted to talk about Asif, but life had gone on without him. Life at The Petal, at least. Chanté's life? Unfortunately, not as much.

The bus pulled along the curb, and Chanté found herself scanning the streets near the club, looking for Asif or his car or something. She sighed when she came up empty. "I'll see you tonight, Miss Francine."

"Okay, girl. Make that money."

Chanté smiled and jogged down the stairs.

"Girl, if you don't use the right exit!" Miss Francine called.

"Bye!"

She darted down the alleyway to the fire door and pounded on it, pulling at the small handle under the lock just in case it was unlocked. It wasn't.

"Good evening, Chanté."

"Hi, Stevie. How's the crowd tonight?"

"Dry," he said with a roll of his eyes. "The dancers' locker room isn't, though," he whispered.

"Oh."

She'd always relied on Angie and Stevie to give her a heads-up on the club temperature so she could adjust the tip calculator in her head, but since she'd become a dancer, she used their judgment to decide if she would wade into the locker room she'd spent over a year dreaming of entering or not.

Tonight, she decided she would not. She kicked the doorstop out of the way as she entered the waitresses' locker room. She shimmied out of her winter clothes, kicked off her boots, and then stepped into her heels. She was swiping glitter body lotion on her exposed flesh when Angie pushed inside.

"You know you could get ready in the bathroom, right?"

"I could, but I'm not. How's the crowd?"

"For us, slow. For y'all, still slow," Angie laughed.

Chanté laughed right along with her. She still found it strange to imagine that very little had actually changed in the past two months. Her new job came with a learning curve, but what new job didn't? She and Angie still caught up quickly before and after their shifts. They still found a few minutes to hang out near the bar and watch the other girls dance. And even though she was a dancer now, Chanté still changed in the waitresses' locker room more often than not because she felt most comfortable here.

She was getting more comfortable on stage and on the floor. There were so many new things to learn and do that every night, at least for a few minutes, she managed to forget Asif.

She pushed out into the hallway and ran straight into Joi.

"Girl, I been looking for you."

"My shift just started," Chanté said.

"And you already got a customer. Come on." Joi grabbed Chanté's hand and walked her down the hall toward the VIP rooms.

"Oh my god," Chanté breathed, jogging carefully in her heels as all of her bounced and jiggled. "I have a VIP?"

Joi stopped in front of the red room and turned to her with a smile.

"I don't know if I'm ready for this. Can someone else do it?" Chanté hissed.

Joi reached out to brush a finger across Chanté's cheek. "You don't have to do anything you don't want to do, but he asked for you specifically."

"He did?"

Joi nodded.

"Who?"

Instead of answering, Joi turned the knob on the red room and pushed the door open.

Chanté knew before she turned to look in the room who it would be. It wasn't just the look in Joi's eyes; it was that crackling feeling of electricity over her skin that she associated with Asif.

A feeling she'd been missing.

Joi's mouth brushed Chanté's ear. "The offer still stands," she said and brushed past her, walking back down the hallway.

For the past two months, Chanté had often felt Joi watching her, and Chanté had often found herself watching Joi. But it was difficult to let herself want Joi without thinking of Asif. It was as if Asif — the real man and the memory of him — was standing in the middle of Chanté and the world.

And the worst part was that she didn't hate having him there.

She walked into the red room.

He was sitting on the same couch where they'd sat

to watch Joi, but when Chanté closed the door, there was only just the two of them.

"Where have you been?" she asked. Her voice was oddly calm.

"That's not the first thing I thought you'd ask me," he said.

That wasn't the first thing Chanté had planned to ask Asif if he ever had the audacity to show his face in this club again. She'd dreamed about this reunion nearly every night since he'd disappeared. Sometimes, she'd imagined taking off a heel and beating him with it. Sometimes, she just dissolved into tears. And more than once, she'd imagined dragging him to bed and cussing him out while they finally had sex.

They had sex in all of these scenarios, actually.

But apparently, in reality, she was much more composed.

"Where have you been?"

"I can't tell you that."

"Why did you leave?"

He sighed. "I can't… I can't tell you that, either."

"Well, what the fuck can you tell me?" she asked, throwing her arms out, flailing physically and emotionally.

"I missed you."

"Obviously. Who wouldn't miss me?" she said, her voice cracking the tiniest bit.

Asif shook his head and chuckled. His smile was as

perfect as the last time she'd seen him. But he looked sad.

"You aren't going to stay, are you?"

Her heart broke when he didn't stop shaking his head.

"So why'd you come back?"

"To say goodbye. You deserve a goodbye."

"Of course." Chanté finally cried.

"Don't," Asif breathed, standing from the couch and rushing to her. He wrapped his arms around her, which only made her cry harder. "Don't cry over me. I promise you that I'm not worth it."

"Of course, you're not, but my bank account really liked you," Chanté lied, laughing through her tears.

Asif pressed his mouth to her temple. He pushed her back against the wall, and she sighed at the feeling of being crushed between the wall and his body. It made her feel safe. Asif made Chanté feel safe even though she barely knew him, and he apparently didn't plan to stick around. Of course.

He held her until she stopped crying, whispering soft words to her, murmuring them in soft kisses into her hair.

"I'm so fucking mad at you," she whispered.

"You should be."

"I had plans for your money."

"Just my money?" he teased.

Chanté lifted her head to glare at him.

He ignored the daggers she was shooting him to wipe away the tracks of her tears from her cheeks.

"You'll never know," she whispered.

He laughed. "Sure. If you say so. Wanna take some more of my money?"

"I'm listening."

"Joi said you haven't had a VIP customer yet."

"I'm working up to it."

Asif dipped his head and kissed her lightly. "Work up to it with me," he whispered and licked her lips.

Chanté shuddered and opened her mouth to him, moaning when their tongues touched. She wrapped her arms around his waist and pulled him forward, wanting him as close as he could get without getting her fired. Or maybe close enough to get her fired.

"Touching the dancers isn't allowed," she moaned against his lips.

"Yep. There's a sign," he said, still kissing her. His hands cupped her face and moved to her neck and down her chest.

Chanté let out a keening moan when his big hands cupped her breasts, and his fingers pinched her nipples. "That's definitely against Petal rules."

Asif nodded as his mouth followed his hands.

"Oh god," Chanté groaned, her body shuddering when his mouth covered her hard nipple through the mesh crop top she was wearing.

"Probably illegal, actually," she hissed, pulling the

ponytail holder from his small bun and digging her fingers into his hair.

His hands kept moving, pressing into the muscles at her back, digging into her hips, and then pushing her legs apart as he sank to his knees on the floor. "I didn't see anything about this," he whispered against her belly button.

Chanté's abdominal muscles jumped as Asif's tongue dipped inside her navel, but it was the way he was looking up her body at her that was the worst.

The best.

A lot.

"I don't remember hearing anything about it," she said because she hadn't. It wasn't a lie. It was lie-adjacent. Plausible deniability. Or whatever.

Asif's hands were massaging the backs of her thighs, and that felt almost as good as his mouth on her breasts; dancing worked muscles she didn't even know she had.

"Let me say goodbye, Chanté," he whispered and then licked a path along her stomach following the top of her thong bikini.

"Is this how you say goodbye?"

"To you? Yes."

"Do you want to?"

"No. I mean, yes. I want to eat you out until you can't stand anymore. I want to drown in your pussy. I want to make a home right here between your legs. But no, I don't want to say goodbye."

Chanté lifted her left leg and placed her foot on his shoulder. She could feel his breath on her inner thigh, and it make her pussy clench.

She smiled when he saw it.

"I thought you might sell it," he said, touching the anklet he'd given her.

"I thought about it. That thing could pay for a whole fucking year of college."

"But you didn't?"

She dug her fingers deeper into his hair and scratched at his scalp.

Asif closed his eyes and moaned as a satisfied smile lifted his face. He was beautiful.

"I wanted to have a piece of you," she admitted.

His face fell, and she could tell that whatever he was about to say would only make them both sad, so she didn't give him the chance. She hooked her left leg over his shoulder and pulled his mouth between her legs.

She let Asif say goodbye.

And he did. He pushed her bottoms to the side and tasted her in soft licks and hard pulls of his lips. He mumbled words she couldn't hear but understood nonetheless into her pussy. He made her come with his mouth and drank up her release, and then jumped back in to make her come again.

Asif ate Chanté out until she couldn't stand, just like he promised, but he didn't stay, like said he wouldn't. He might have said goodbye, but Chanté hadn't.

She decided sometime between the third and fourth orgasms that she just wasn't ready to let Asif go.

---

epilogue

---

Asif had one more pit stop before he left the Midwest, and he'd been dreading it for the past twenty-four hours, once the reality that he'd probably never see Chanté again had settled like a heavy weight in his bones.

The regional headquarters of The Agency was in a nondescript Chicago strip mall that looked as if it was one bad shopping season away from being shut down. Asif had left The Petal and started driving straight here, worried that if he didn't leave Cleveland immediately, he might not at all. He'd arrived in the middle of the night and checked into a safehouse The Agency ran that looked like a cheap motel. It felt like one too.

He spent a little more time than usual getting dressed that morning, knowing that how he presented himself mattered almost as much as the topic at hand.

"Good morning, sir," the receptionist said as soon as Asif walked into the door. Receptionist was an odd cover for an agent responsible for at least three assassinations in the last year, but allocating human assets wasn't his job, and he never wanted that kind of responsibility. "Please sign in."

Asif nodded and slid his hand into the biometric scanner, waiting for the red light to turn green.

If it didn't, there was probably a sniper somewhere with a gun trained on his head, ready to take him out. But the light did flash green.

"She's waiting for you in her office," the receptionist said.

"Thanks."

The staircase behind the receptionist's desk seemed to lead to an empty second story, but when Asif made it to the top step, he found a wall of heavy metal doors and a security guard sitting at a small desk, reading a newspaper.

Asif could only see one of his hands at first. He imagined that the other was holding a firearm under the desk, aimed at center mass. But then his hand moved into focus, and the metal doors swung open. The buzz of the office behind the desk overwhelmed Asif for a few seconds as it did every time.

There were two rows of desks on either side of the room with a clear pathway across the floor to an office. Asif took a deep breath to calm his nerves as he set his path for that office. Through the windows, he could see her sitting at her desk, reading from a folder in front of her. He wondered if those were his mission briefs. He hoped they weren't.

He knocked on the door and waited.

"Come in."

He pulled the door open and walked inside. The sounds of the outer room faded to almost nothing. Her office was quiet, almost serene even.

"Have a seat," she said, still reading from the folder. She continued to read while he sat and waited. Her door opened, and a man he didn't recognize entered with a cup and saucer and a juice glass on a tray.

"Green tea," he said, placing the cup in front of the woman, "and cranberry juice," he said, putting the glass on a coaster in front of Asif.

"Thank you."

The man nodded and then hustled out of the room.

The woman waited until she heard the door click shut to lift her head from her reading. She assessed him with a squinting glare, peering at him through her glasses as if she could see through him. Asif wasn't entirely certain that she couldn't. She finally spoke.

"You drove all night?" she asked.

"Didn't think there was any reason to wait."

"Hmmm. I heard your target is in the wind?"

Asif nodded. "We got her father and brother, though."

"Hmmm," she hummed again.

"I assigned Smith to look after her."

"And you think he's ready for that?"

"I do."

"This will also get him out of your hair for a while," she said.

Asif pressed his lips together.

She took her glasses from her face and smiled at him. "How are you, beta?"

"Tired, maa, but okay."

"You should rest between missions," Asif's mother said.

"I don't remember you taking breaks."

She scoffed at him. "I had you. I took many breaks. You always forget."

"Maybe."

"Are you leaving right away, or will you have time to have dinner with your parents? Your father would like to see you."

Asif nodded his head. "I know. I'm going home to see him as soon as I leave here."

"Good. Good. Let's get your debriefing out of the way, then."

Asif sat up straighter in his chair, and his back twinged with a sharp pain. He'd put his body through a lot in the last twelve hours, and though he didn't regret any of it, he did feel every minute of those hours, physically and emotionally. And while emotional turmoil often felt like the name of the spy game, he couldn't afford to be unstable in front of The Agency head, and not just because she was his mother.

"Tell me about the waitress," she said.

Asif reached for his glass of juice and took a sip. "What would you like to know?"

His mother smiled faintly before putting her glasses back on her face and picking up the folder from her desk.

"'Agent seems particularly attached to mark,'" she read.

"She wasn't the mark," Asif corrected, blurting the words out before he could stop himself.

His mother lifted her eyes over her glasses and stared at him for a second before continuing.

"'She could be a liability. Only time will tell.'" She finished reading from that page and turned until she found another. "Accounting says that you spent nearly six thousand dollars in a single week on the waitress. Much of this money without prior authorization." She finished reading, took her glasses off, and looked at him again.

Asif clasped his hands together between his legs, forcing himself not to respond. He'd already made one mistake.

"I'm assuming that she was not a liability."

"No, ma'am. She was actually quite valuable."

"Clearly. Should I be worried for you?" she asked.

Asif blinked at her, parsing the specific wording of her question. His mother was nothing if not precise. She was also dangerous. As a child, Asif had believed his mother's cover, telling everyone who asked that she was a flight attendant, that's why she was always away. He hadn't gotten clearance to find out what his mother did for a living until he was eighteen, and immediately, he'd known what he wanted to do with his life.

All new agents researched Agency history but reading about his mother's exploits in the 1970s, '80s, and early '90s had been a surreal experience. On the one hand, he'd been in awe of everything she'd accomplished and proud of her beyond measure. But on the other hand, when he charted the peaks and valleys of her career alongside the timeline of his life, he couldn't help but note the commendation for uncovering and preventing a terrorist attack that coincided with his sixth birthday. While he'd been graduating from elementary school, his mother had been in Ireland, infiltrating a radical separatist organization. It wasn't as if Asif had been alone. Asif's father was loving and attentive, and on a day-to-day basis, sometimes Asif hadn't even known to miss his mother because her travels were just a fact of life.

But she had been gone more than she'd been home — and knowing why didn't actually make Asif feel any better about all the parts of his life she'd missed. It made their relationship awkward in a way he was still struggling to deal with. He'd spent so much of his life without his mother. He understood that her time away was as much to keep him and his father safe as to do her job well. He was working to understand that and forgive, but he wasn't there yet. Every conversation was laced with meaning and a touch of danger and so much responsibility. Everyone knew that Asif was Madiha's son, and ever since he'd been recruited, Asif hadn't been able to shake the feeling that people were watching him, waiting for him to fuck up. But he couldn't fuck up. Of all the things he refused to do, marring his mother's legacy wasn't an option.

"There's nothing to worry about," he said.

"We all say that," she said. "But I would not be doing my job if I did not take the chance to remind you that what we do is dangerous."

"I know."

She raised a hand to silence him. "Our jobs are dangerous and unpredictable. I understand the impulse to reach out for something that seems safe and stable. But we must never forget that in our search for stability, we can put others at risk."

Asif clasped his hands tighter together. He knew that, and he'd spent nearly every moment with Chanté terrified of just that possibility. "I know," he rasped in a suddenly dry voice. What Asif wanted to tell his mother was that she didn't have to worry about him putting Chanté in danger because he knew better than most what it was like to live in the wake of a spy's life. To wait for them, to need them and not even know what time zone they were in. He wouldn't put Chanté or anyone through that. He knew what living with a spy had done to him. He'd seen what his father had endured.

He couldn't.

"Can I ask a favor?"

"You can ask me anything, and I will always consider your request."

He nodded. "I'd like to send the waitress…Chanté a portion of my next paycheck."

He was giving away so much in this moment, but he didn't care. "She was instrumental in my ability to close this case," he offered as a halfhearted cover.

His mother considered him in silence for a few long minutes before nodding. "If you file your formal request, I will figure out how to get the money to her without exposing your identity."

"Thank you," Asif said.

"You're welcome. And you should be very proud of yourself."

Asif dipped his head forward and nodded, the sting of tears burning his eyes.

"I am proud of you," his mother whispered.

three months later

"HEY, YOU WORKING TONIGHT?" Kenny asked.

"Nope," Chanté said without looking up from her laptop, "tomorrow."

"Damn."

She turned from her computer to look at him now. "Why? You tryna have some company?"

Kenny rolled his eyes. "No, I was going to ask you to bring back some wings."

"Those wings are not that good."

"Yes, they are," he said, plopping down on the couch next to her. "What are you doing?"

"Nothing much, just searching some online forums for some stuff."

"What stuff… God, you better not be hacking into the IRS or something."

"Ew, why would I do that? Their servers are ghetto. No art in it at all. I'm just trying to figure out where the fuck that scholarship I told you about is from."

"Why do you care?" Kenny asked. "An extra seven thousand dollars that paid for all your summer classes and a new computer. You don't even have to work at the club if you don't want to."

"I don't, but I am. And I'm not trying to give the money back or anything. I'm just saying, where the fuck did it come from?"

"Well…?"

"So, I did have to hack into the university's financial aid servers."

"Oh my god, we're going to get kicked out of school."

"Oh my god, it's my account. I just needed the routing and account numbers for the transfer."

"Okay?"

"And that should have given me all the information I needed, but the routing number led to some bank in fucking Norway, and the account number was fake as hell anyway."

"Okay, that's weird," Kenny breathed, leaning into her side to look at her computer screen.

"Very. I've been searching for the source and ended up on this doomsday prepper conspiracy theory forum. If we get kicked out of our apartment, it'll be because of this site. These people are terrifying. Definitely on some domestic terrorist shit."

"You better have found something after all this."

Chanté shrugged. "Not yet, just these vague ass posts about The Agency."

"What agency?"

"*The* Agency," she said.

Kenny turned to her and frowned. "That sounds

incredibly fake. Can you bring some wings home tomorrow?"

"Yeah, sure."

"Thanks, roomie," he said and stood from the couch.

Also by Katrina Jackson

**Welcome to Sea Port**

From Scratch

Inheritance

Small Town Secrets

Her Christmas Cookie

**The Spies Who Loved Her**

Pink Slip

Private Eye

Bang & Burn

New Year, New We

His Only Valentine

Bright Lights

**Erotic Accommodations**

Room for Three?

Neighborly

**Love At Last**

Every New Year

**Heist Holidays**

Grand Theft N.Y.E.

**The Family**